D0261630

EA
07/15

Gila Monster

A stagecoach is winding its way towards the small town of Medicine Bend when it is attacked by outlaws. However the coach's passengers manage to beat them off. This unusual array of characters – the new town marshal Wade Calvin, insurance salesman Taber, and Miss Jowett, on her way to care for her relatives – thus find their lives intertwined.

As the new arrivals settle in, the outlaws' vicious leader 'Gila' Goad hears news of the botched robbery from his base in a disused silver mining camp in the surrounding hills. Named after the deadly Gila lizard he keeps as a pet, Goad is brutal and unpredictable. He learns of Calvin's presence in town and believes he is the same man who once imprisoned him. Goad is determined to get his revenge.

When Miss Jowett's young relatives are kidnapped, Calvin knows the race to find the outlaws is on. He must take the fight deep into the hills as he searches for Goad and his camp, and the stolen children – before it is too late.

Gila Monster

Colin Bainbridge

A Black Horse Western

ROBERT HALE · LONDON

© Colin Bainbridge 2015
First published in Great Britain 2015

ISBN 978-0-7198-1574-4

Robert Hale Limited
Clerkenwell House
Clerkenwell Green
London EC1R 0HT

www.halebooks.com

Typeset by
Derek Doyle & Associates, Shaw Heath
Printed and bound in Great Britain by
CPI Antony Rowe, Chippenham and Eastbourne

CHAPTER ONE

'Goin' kinda slow, ain't it?'

The remark was made by the dapper-looking individual in a corner seat of the stagecoach. Since no-one bothered to reply, he leaned forward and peered through the window at a barren landscape of sagebrush, rocky outcrops and scattered stunted cacti.

'Guess it's uphill,' he volunteered.

He would have liked to stretch his legs but the man opposite didn't look the type to make way. He was lean and his skin was drawn tight over his features; in his long, black frock-coat, he resembled a stick insect. The other traveller was a fashionably dressed lady of middle years.

The stagecoach lumbered along, swaying slightly

from side to side and bringing its passengers up with a jolt when the wheels struck a rock. The atmosphere inside the stage was heavy and he would have opened a window if it hadn't been for the dust that hung in the torpid air outside. If he twisted his head and peered upwards, he could see the boot of the shotgun guard resting on the roof. He was beginning to feel drowsy so it came as something of a shock when the silence was broken by a voice and he realized that the lady was addressing him.

'I hope you don't mind my asking, but I was wondering if you are new to the West as I am. It's Mr Taber, isn't it? I heard someone call you by that name at the last relay station.'

'That is correct, ma'am, and yes, I am new to these parts.'

The lady smiled and without preamble began to introduce herself. 'I'm Miss Jowett. I'm on my way to join my nephew. You might know of him.' She was suddenly confused. 'Oh, of course not! You just told me you're new here. How silly of me!'

'Seems like we're both newcomers,' he replied. She smiled and he continued: 'Is your nephew a citizen of Medicine Bend?'

'Oh, no. He owns a ranch a little way out of town called the Sycamore.' The lady fell silent and he detected a certain awkwardness.

'It's rather sad. His wife died quite recently. I've come to help take charge of his children.'

Taber glanced at the man opposite. Although he remained aloof from the conversation, it seemed to him that he had shown a flicker of interest at the lady's words. There were a few more moments of silence before she resumed:

'Might I ask if you're visiting?'

'You could say that,' he replied, 'although I intend stayin' for a while. I'm an insurance salesman.'

'Insurance?'

'Yes. Since they discovered silver in the hills, Medicine Bend is *the* up-and-coming place. Folks need security, and the Armitas Company can offer it to them. At a very modest premium, might I add.'

The man opposite stirred and seemed about to say something, but instead he turned to the window and glanced out. When he looked back it seemed to Taber that there was a thoughtful look in his eyes.

'Yes,' Taber resumed. 'Small savings are the foundation of security.'

As if in response to his comment, the stagecoach suddenly lurched and then began to speed up.

'What the devil?' he muttered.

There was a cry of alarm from the lady as the

coach continued to gather pace. It began to swing from side to side and the passengers clutched at anything that might offer some support. The woman screamed again. Suddenly the man opposite came to life.

'Get down!' he snapped. At the same moment there came the crackle of gunfire.

'What's goin' on?' Taber began, but the man's only response was to grab him by the collar of his coat and drag him to the floor where the woman already cowered. The man opened the window and, drawing a sawn-off shotgun from the recesses of his coat, began to fire. Shots were ringing out from on top of the coach and Taber at last realized that they were under attack. Dragging himself along the floor, he got to his feet to side-step the woman before flinging open the opposite window. Two riders were bearing down fast on the coach. He looked across at the man in the black frock-coat.

'Have you got a gun?' he demanded.

The man in the frock coat stopped shooting for a moment. His expression was doubtful, but he reached quickly and threw a six-gun across to the insurance salesman. Taber grabbed it and turned to the window.

One of the riders had got ahead of the other and

had almost caught up to the flying stagecoach. Leaning slightly out of the window, Taber took aim and fired. The man flung up his arms and fell backwards as his horse thundered on. Bullets flew by Taber's head and he pulled back hastily inside the coach. He waited for a few moments and then glanced outside again. The second rider had fallen back but through the dust Taber could now see that there were others. He began shooting, although there wasn't much chance that he would hit anybody.

The stage continued at a breakneck speed, swaying and swerving, till it suddenly skewed and swung sideways. For what seemed like an eternity it seemed to hang suspended in the air, then over it went with a rending and crashing that rang like thunder in his ears, drowning out the sounds of shooting and the screams of the hapless woman. Taber felt himself flying through the air and he landed with a crash that sent a burst of pain surging through his body. For a moment he lay stunned, but consciousness quickly returned and he saw that the door had opened and he had been flung clear. The coach lay with its wheels spinning on the side nearest to him. The horses were braying and struggling in the traces. The driver lay supine at a little distance, but the shotgun guard still had his rifle in his hand and was continuing to fire.

From the opposite side a figure emerged from the wreckage and, lying athwart the upturned stage, resumed shooting with the sawn-off gun. Dazed and confused, Taber struggled to his feet and looked back down the trail. It was hard to make anything out very clearly through the clouds of dust, but he could see a little knot of riders who seemed to have come to a halt. Shots still rang out but they were sporadic. When he looked closer, he could discern what looked like bodies of men and horses scattered at intervals along the trail. The shotgun guard and the man in the frock coat were continuing to fire and when he became aware that his hand still clutched the six-gun, he pointed it at the horsemen and fired. There was an answering salvo and then the horsemen began to move away, riding at a canter till they were well back down the trail before turning and riding away into the shelter of the sagebrush. For a few moments longer he continued to watch the scene, gathering himself together as he did so, when he was brought to attention by a voice calling:

'Help me get these broncs out of the traces!'

He looked over his shoulder to see the driver struggling with the team of horses. In a few seconds he was joined by the shotgun guard. He was about to lend his support when his attention was caught by the sight of the man in the black frock coat as he struggled to drag something out of the coach door. The head of the woman appeared and Taber was relieved to hear her sobs. He ran round the side of the coach to assist and in a few more moments they succeeded in lifting the lady from the coach. The man carried the woman to a nearby rock and propped her shoulders against it.

'I'll be right back, lady,' he said.

He gestured to Taber and they helped free the horses. When they had done this, Taber and the man in the frock coat joined the driver and shotgun guard, who were standing together with their hands on their hips, drawing in deep breaths of air. The sun was high and they were sweating with all their efforts. The man in the frock coat turned to Taber.

'You did good,' he said. 'I never figured you to handle a gun.'

'I didn't always sell insurance,' Taber replied. At his words the driver and guard exchanged glances before suddenly breaking into a laugh.

'Hell,' the driver said, 'You sure chose the right time to take it up again.'

Taber stood silent for a moment and then, seeing the irony of the situation, he too began laughing. He was aware that he was trembling and he knew that the laughter was partly born of relief. Only the man in the black frock coat remained silent till their laughter came to a halt.

'I guess we'd better get our backs into getting the coach upright,' he said. Taber looked closely at him.

'I never did catch your name,' he remarked.

The man turned to him. 'Calvin,' he replied, 'Wade Calvin. Glad to make your acquaintance.' His words seemed to produce a reaction on the part of the driver and shotgun guard.

'Wade Calvin?' the driver said. 'Ain't I heard that name before?'

The shotgun guard was scrutinizing him closely. 'You ain't the Wade Calvin that cleaned out Fromberg?'

'If you care to put it that way. Certainly I was the town marshal for a time.'

The driver and guard exchanged glances. 'Hell, no wonder those varmints decided to call off the attack,' the guard said, ignoring the obvious fact that they couldn't possibly have seen who was travelling inside the stagecoach.

'You undervalue yourself. It was down to you both that we fought 'em off.'

The guard stroked his stubbled chin. 'I'd sure like to get even with those varmints,' he said.

The driver shrugged. 'What are you doin' in these parts?' he asked Calvin.

'By all accounts, Medicine Bend is a little short of law and order. I think what just happened here tends to prove it. I'm the new marshal.'

'Isn't there a marshal already?' Taber asked.

'Nope. There was, but apparently he decided he'd had enough.'

Taber gave a wan smile. 'Looks to me like you could maybe make use of some insurance yourself,' he said, feeling slightly nonplussed.

'I wouldn't be able to afford the premiums,' Calvin replied.

'Well, it's sure good to have you along,' the guard said. 'This isn't the first occasion the stage has been targeted. It's about time somethin' was done about it. Those low-down coyotes owe me.'

'Right now I think we'd better see to the lady and then get outta here,' Calvin replied.

The driver nodded and, as he and the shotgun guard resumed their seats, Calvin and Taber returned to where they had left the woman. She was looking worn and dishevelled, but already she seemed to have regained some of her composure.

'I'm sorry about what happened,' Calvin said. 'It ain't usual.'

13

Taber glanced at him. From what he had been saying about Medicine Bend, he had gained the impression that it was far from unusual.

'What will we do now?' she replied.

'Don't concern yourself. We'll have that coach upright directly and then we'll be on our way again.'

'Maybe you'd like some water?' Taber suggested. She nodded and he reached into his jacket to produce a small flask.

'Hold on to it,' he said when she had taken a drink and offered it him back. 'Right now, we've got work to do.'

Way back along the trail, the men who had attacked the stagecoach were counting the cost of the enterprise. Three of their number were missing and there was little doubt that they were dead.

'Gila ain't gonna like this, Strawson,' one of them said. Strawson, the leader of their little party, turned to him with a snarl.

'Shut yer mouth!' he snapped. The man's words grated on him. He was stating the obvious, and he would be held responsible. Gila was not the sort of person you wanted to upset. He was unpredictable and strange, as evidenced by the name he had come to be known by. Gila wasn't his real name; that was

Goad. He had earned the sobriquet from the fact that he kept a Gila monster as a pet.

'We could have dealt with the shotgun guard,' he said. 'He was just plumb lucky. But he weren't the only one shootin' back.'

'It ain't happened before,' another man commented.

'Never mind any of that. The point is, what do we do about it?'

'Leave that to Gila.'

Strawson was inclined to do just that. On the other hand. . . . He might at least be able to modify the failure.

'How many people do you reckon were returnin' fire?' he queried.

'One . . . maybe a couple,' replied the man who had originally spoken.

'No – I figure there were more'n that.'

The others fell silent for a few moments till another man spoke up again. 'I reckon Strawson's right. There were more than two of the varmints; I'd say three or four at least. Maybe they even planted those guns.'

'Could be. They must be gettin' wise after the number of robberies we've carried out.'

'Well, they ain't gonna get away with it,' Strawson

concluded. 'Deliberately arrangin' to have gunmen along as passengers just ain't fair play. We'll tell Gila that. Don't worry, he'll make sure we hit back – and real hard this time.'

His words seemed to rally the men. Without taking the conversation further, they climbed back into leather and carried on riding.

The stagecoach was nearing the town of Medicine Bend. For the hapless passengers inside, it was a rougher journey even than usual. The stage had taken a battering and they felt the impact of every slight bump in the road. The driver strained his eyes, seeking to avoid the worst obstacles, and suddenly he jerked to attention. At the same moment the shotgun guard swung up his rifle.

'More trouble?' he snapped.

Coming towards them was a group of three riders. Suddenly the driver's face broke into a grin. 'Hey, ain' that old Hurlock?' he said.

The guard laughed. 'Sure is. Looks like some folks got worried about the delay. I'll bet you a dollar to a dime that the other two are from the Sycamore.'

As the riders drew close, the driver hauled on the brake and brought the coach to a halt. 'Howdy, Hurlock,' the guard said.

The man addressed was small and wiry. 'Looking at that coach,' he said. 'I'd say you ran into some trouble.' Just then the door of the stage opened and Calvin stepped out.

'If it's the lady you're lookin' for,' he said, 'she's fine.'

'We're from the Sycamore,' one of the other horsemen said. 'We're here to escort Miss Jowett to the ranch.'

As if to confirm Calvin's comment, she appeared in the doorframe and stepped down, with the assistance of Taber. She was still somewhat shaken, but had regained a measure of composure. She looked up at the riders, but she didn't recognize her nephew.

'Howdy, ma'am,' the man who had previously spoken said, taking off his Stetson and then replacing it. 'My name is Whitman and this is McNab. I'm the foreman of the Sycamore. Mr Jowett sends his apologies that he wasn't able to meet you in person. If you like to carry on just a little further, we have a buggy waitin' back in Medicine Bend for your convenience.'

'That will do nicely,' the lady replied.

During this exchange, Hurlock was looking in turn at Calvin and Taber.

17

'Well,' he said, 'I guess one of you must be the new marshal. Leastways, he was due to arrive on this stage-coach.'

Calvin nodded. 'I sure appreciate the welcomin' committee,' he said. 'I'm Calvin, the new marshal.'

The oldster licked his lips and grinned. 'Looks to me like you already met with a welcomin' committee,' he responded.

'Yeah. Some of 'em are lyin' back along the trail. When we get to Medicine Bend, you can roust out the undertaker.'

'That's easy done. You might say I'm his assistant.'

Calvin glanced at Miss Jowett. 'Sorry,' he said. 'I had no business to mention such matters in front of a lady.'

In reply she smiled sadly. 'I'm not offended,' she said. 'I'm just very tired. Could we leave the explanations till later and complete the journey?'

'Of course.' Calvin turned to the Sycamore riders. 'You go on ahead and get things ready. Is it far from town to the Sycamore?'

'Nope. Just a few miles.'

'Do you think you can carry on or would you prefer to put up for a night at the local hotel?' Calvin asked Miss Jowett.

'I'll be fine,' she said. 'I think I'd like to get to the

Sycamore just as soon as I can now.' She turned aside and Taber helped her back into the stage.

'OK,' Calvin said, 'Let's get goin'.'

He climbed back inside the coach himself. The shotgun guard put his foot up and the driver cracked his whip. In a few moments the stage had resumed its clattering way.

The hills all around Medicine Bend were pocked by silver mines, but very few of them amounted to anything. A broad band of mineral rock ran through the region and prospectors were constantly attracted by the possibility of discovering a major lode, but only a tiny number of deposits were big enough to merit the construction of a full working mine. Most of the ore was silver, which involved heavy costs and major difficulties to extract. One such undeveloped site bore the name of the Silver Horse Mill and Mining Company, but it amounted to little more than a tunnel and some accompanying shacks and sheds. It was of no use as a mine, but situated deep in a valley of the hills around Medicine Bend, it provided the ideal base for Gila and his gang of outlaws.

Evening had drawn down, and he was sitting astride a chair outside one of the shacks, looking up at a hillside opposite, when the door of the shack

19

opened and a woman emerged. She wore a shift that did little to conceal the outlines of her body, and her legs and feet were bare.

'Why don't you dress properly?' he said.

'Don't you like me in this?' she replied. He took a good look at her, making no effort to conceal his admiration.

'Sure, but some of the boys are around. There's no call to display yourself.'

Her laugh was strangely child-like. 'I can handle them,' she said.

'So can I. That isn't the point.'

She sat on his knee and, kissing his ear, began to whisper in baby talk. 'Speak properly, Lottie. What is it you want?' he said, roughly.

She sat upright. 'I'm getting bored cooped up here. Why do we have to spend so much time in this place? Why can't we go into town?'

He looked at her and put his hand over her breasts. 'Now ain't the time,' he replied.

'What about the ranch then? You told me you were taking over a ranch. What's the use of havin' a ranch if we spend all our time here?'

'The business of the ranch ain't completed yet,' he said. He thought for a moment. 'Maybe a trip into town could be arranged. I think we might manage that. In fact, I was already thinkin' of spendin' some time there.'

She giggled. He removed one hand and began to fumble under her petticoat, running it slowly up the inside of her leg. She bit his lip and whispering something, got to her feet.

'Come on,' she said.

He took a final sip of the whiskey and was about to follow her into the shack when he heard the sound of hoof beats. Looking down the valley, he saw three riders approaching. He recognised them as Strawson and a couple of his companions. Immediately, he sensed something was wrong. When Strawson had set off to carry out the stagecoach robbery, there had been six of them. For a moment he thought of ignoring them, but then changed his mind. He was annoyed, but it looked like something he might need to deal with. Business first, then pleasure. The girl wouldn't be going anywhere. Waiting for just a short while would sharpen both their appetites.

Wade Calvin stood at the window of the room above the marshal's office, which served as his living quarters, and looked down on the bustling street below. The marshal's office was situated at the junction of Main Street and Fourth Street. Just past the junction was the busiest part of town. Together with the usual array of stores and businesses, it boasted three saloons as well as a restaurant and a hotel. Further down were the livery stables, the bank, the Mining Exchange building, and the assay office. Further back, the surrounding hills were ringed with hoists and smelters and other structures in various stages of newness or disrepair. The place was busy with people going about their business. Riders passed up and down, competing for space with wagons and buckboards as well as pedestrians. As he watched, a figure detached itself from the crowd, coming towards him, and he recognized the figure of Hurlock. Slipping on his jacket, he opened the door to his room and clattered down the stairs just as there was a knock on the outer door. He opened it to admit the undertaker's assistant.

'Mornin, Marshal,' Hurlock said, grinning and revealing a mouth bereft of teeth except for a few black and broken stumps, like fallen trees in a damp swamp.

'Mornin',' Calvin replied. He ran his hand through his hair. 'Have you collected those bodies?' he asked.

'Sure thing.'

'I might want to come over and take a look.'

'Sure thing,' Hurlock repeated, 'but you'd better

make it soon.' He paused, still grinning, before adding: 'I don't suppose you've eaten yet?'

'I was just about to find someplace.'

'I can recommend Brown's Eating House.' He paused as if expecting a reply and Calvin obliged.

'Sounds good,' he said. 'Care to join me?'

The two of them stepped outside, Calvin locking the door behind him. They crossed the street, side-stepping a buggy that came round the corner, and entered the café. Apart from a man sitting at one of the tables, the place was quiet. They took a seat by the window as a middle-aged woman with her hair fastened in a snood came over.

'The whole works,' Hurlock said.

'For both of you?'

Calvin looked up. 'Yes,' he nodded, 'and plenty of strong coffee.'

'A speciality of the place,' she replied with a smile.

When she had gone Hurlock turned to Calvin. 'How are you settlin' in?' he said.

'Kinda early to say. I figure to take a good look aroun'. Sure is busy though. Kept me awake durin' the night.'

'That's the way of it. The mines operate in shifts and never close, so the town does the same.'

Calvin glanced out of the window. 'Don't seem to

be too much trouble.'

'How much are you gettin' paid for takin' on the job?' Hurlock replied, at a tangent.

'One hundred dollars a month and room.'

Hurlock grinned again. 'Don't worry, you'll earn every last dime of it. The town might be fairly quiet now, but there's a heap o' trouble brewin' from those outlaws.'

'You mean the ones who attacked the stagecoach?'

'Yeah. They need stoppin'.'

Calvin regarded the little man for a few moments. 'How about you?' he said. 'How are you doin'?'

'What do you mean?'

'Well, how do you feel about your job, for instance? How do you like bein' an undertaker's assistant?'

'Part-time assistant,' Hurlock replied. 'I do a few other jobs about the place.'

'What, like swampin' out at one of the saloons?'

'You got it,' Hurlock replied.

Calvin looked thoughtfully out of the window again before turning back to the oldster.

'I'm goin' to need help sortin' out those outlaw varmints,' he said. 'I figure I'll need a deputy. Maybe more'n one. There'll be risks involved. But how would you fancy takin' on the role?'

Hurlock's eyes opened wider with surprise as the familiar snaggle-toothed grin began to spread across his grizzled features.

'You mean it?' he said.

'I take it you can use a gun?'

'Sure thing! I once rode shotgun for a stage-line. And that ain't all. Why. . . .'

Calvin held up his hand. 'You don't need to go into all that,' he said. 'Just say if you want the job.'

'Hell, yes,' the oldster replied. 'Ain't never been asked somethin' like that before.'

'Consider yourself deputized. We can go through the formalities later and you can pin on your star.'

Hurlock was about to reply but whatever he intended to say remained unspoken as the woman came back with a tray on which were two platters piled high with food. She placed them on the table with due ceremony.

'Coffee comin' right up,' she said.

When she brought the coffee over, she stood for a moment with her hands on her hips. Hurlock looked at her and then seemed to remember something.

'Oh, yes,' he said, 'I should have introduced you. Dolores, this is Wade Calvin, the new Marshal. Calvin, meet Dolores Brown, the proprietor of Brown's Eating House.'

Calvin put his fork down and got to his feet. 'Pleased to meet you, ma'am,' he said.

'I wish you luck,' she replied. 'The last marshal didn't last long; nor the one before that.'

'I aim to stay a while,' Calvin replied.

Hurlock looked up at the woman. 'I'll be assistin' the marshal,' he said. By way of reply, she threw him a quizzical glance.

'Mr Hurlock is goin' to be deputy marshal,' Calvin confirmed.

She continued to look at the oldster and the corners of her mouth twitched. She seemed about to laugh, but it was only for a moment and then her features resumed their customary expression.

'In that case, I wish the same for the both of you,' she said. Hurlock watched her as she made her way back to the kitchen.

'That's a mighty fine lady,' he said, somewhat wistfully. They continued eating in silence till it was suddenly broken by the oldster.

'Hey!' he said. 'This place is right across from the marshal's office. Maybe we could arrange for Dolores to fix us somethin' once in a while.'

Calvin paused and took a drink of coffee. 'You reckon she would do that?'

'Sure. She ain't the type to turn down business.'

Calvin considered the matter. 'Let me get to know the place first,' he said. 'I wouldn't want to rush things.'

'Well, don't leave it too long.'

Calvin glanced at him. Was the oldster holding a torch for Dolores? Or was he just thinking of his stomach? If it was the former, it wasn't any of his concern, but he reckoned it was the latter. He finished his plate of food, wiping the last traces of gravy with a hunk of bread, and Hurlock did likewise. As they got to their feet Dolores reappeared and Hurlock tentatively reached into his jacket. Calvin put a restraining hand on his arm.

'I'll pay,' he said.

As they were about to leave, he looked around the room. The man who had been sitting at the table was no longer there.

'I didn't see him leave,' he remarked to Hurlock.

The oldster shrugged. 'Me neither.' They went out into the sunlight.

'Did you recognize him?' Calvin said.

The oldster squinted up at him. 'Who? The man in the café? Nope, I didn't recognize him. It's a big town. People come and go. Why should I?'

'No reason,' Calvin replied.

'Why do you ask?'

'I don't know. There was something about him, something vaguely familiar.'

He looked up and down the street. If anything, it was busier than when they had entered the eating-house. His thoughts were interrupted by Hurlock.

'You want to go take a look at those corpses?'

Calvin thought for a moment. 'No, I got another idea. Take a look around. What do you see?'

'A lot of folk comin' and goin',' Hurlock replied.

'Yes, and too many of 'em carryin' side irons. I assume there's a printer in Medicine Bend?'

'Sure thing. Down at the newspaper offices. Why do you want to go there?'

'To print off an ordinance bannin' the wearin' of guns. Your first job can be puttin' the notices up around town.'

Hurlock grunted and spat into the dust. 'You can print as many notices as you like,' he replied. 'Gettin' folks to take any heed is a different matter.'

Calvin looked down at the little man. 'That's what we're here for,' he said. 'To make sure that they do.'

CHAPTER TWO

Gila emerged from the shack he shared with the woman, and began walking. After listening to Strawson's story, he had taken out his annoyance on her, but he felt little sense of relief. He had received further information from one of his men who had observed something significant in Brown's Eating House. It seemed a new marshal had taken over. That needed thinking about. He strode quickly, devoured by a mixture of emotions he couldn't name, till he came to what had started as the entrance to a tunnel but had never been developed. It was more of a cave and, stooping slightly, he went inside. When his angry feelings tended to overwhelm him, it was his chosen spot away from everybody else where he could try to gather himself together. The process took time, but when he eventually did so, his overwrought condition was almost always succeeded by a corresponding sense of calm. It was then that he tended to do most of the planning concerning the various activities with which his gang was occupied. The tunnel didn't extend very far back but its gloom seemed to act as a kind of balm on his agitated nerves.

Sitting with his back against the rock and his hands across his knees, he reached into his pocket and, pulling on a pair of leather gloves, produced the lizard which was his companion on these occasions. Holding it in the palm of one hand, he stroked its head with the other. Gradually he began to feel better. His anger subsided and soon became a desire for revenge. The fact that some members of his gang had been killed didn't worry him at all. It was more to do with his own reputation and a sense of resentment that nobody seemed to have recognized just how important a figure he was. Well, it was time to change all that. Something needed to be done, something more daring than another stagecoach hold-up or rustling cattle to hide away in the hills. It shouldn't be long, too, till he had the Sycamore ranch under his control. He would carry on with those operations anyway. Certainly the stage-line needed to be taught a lesson. But above and beyond that, he needed to assert his power, and that would involve doing something on a bigger scale altogether. If what he had heard from one of his men was right, and a new marshal had arrived in Medicine Bend, now was the time to do it. But what could it be? Suddenly he had the answer: the bank in Medicine Bend. At the end of the month it would be swollen with the money used to pay the miners as well as with the takings from the general businesses of the town. It was the obvious answer, and with all that loot he could really begin to think about extending his little empire. So far he had been operating on too small a scale. Now the time had come to really assert himself, and it was hard luck on the citizens of Medicine Bend and anyone else who got in his way once he got started. Feeling completely restored, he stroked the lizard once more before transferring it back to his pocket.

Marshal Calvin stood in the doorframe of his office and observed the scene on the street. As usual, the place was bustling, but it was peaceful. He had been in town for two days and nothing had happened. He had paid a call on the local saloons; they were rowdy, but nothing more, and that was to be expected.

Even the appearance at various places of his notice banning the wearing of weapons had not brought about any adverse reaction. It seemed to be working. Already he had noticed that fewer men were carrying guns, and on the few occasions he had directly admonished anybody, they had been compliant. He glanced over his shoulder. A number of weapons were in a cupboard under lock and key, waiting for their owners to collect them. He should have been satisfied, but instead he felt uneasy. There was something ominous about the lack of action. As he thought abut the matter, he came to two conclusions. Either he had been misled, or something big was brewing. The situation was not new to him, and if he had to choose which of the two options was the most likely, experience told him it would be the second.

Out of the corner of his eye he saw someone approaching. It was Hurlock coming down the street, carrying some papers in his hand. As he came up he gave his usual grin and held out one of the papers.

'Looks like we hit pay dirt,' he said.

Calvin took the paper and looked at it. It was a Wanted poster for a man named Wilton, wanted for murder and robbery. Beneath the offer of reward the face of the outlaw stared up at him.

'Are you sure this is one of 'em?' Calvin said, referring to the corpses Hurlock had brought in.

'He ain't lookin' quite so perky, but I'd warrant it's him.' The oldster looked at the marshal and the grin faded from his features. 'Somethin' wrong?' he asked.

'If you're right about the identification, it means we got more on our hands with those thievin' hold-up varmints than just dealin' with a bunch of local desperadoes. That man is well-known in more than one territory, and he's a known associate of some of the most hardened owlhoots around. Yes, I'd say we got our hands full.'

'You want to take a look for yourself?'

'Nope. Go right ahead and bury 'em.' Hurlock was about to move when Calvin thought of another question. 'You said there'd been a number of hold-ups before this one?' he enquired.

'Yeah. From what I've heard, the stage company could go out of business. There ain't been a stage in or out of town since you arrived. They're lookin' for more shotgun guards, but nobody seems keen to volunteer.'

'Those varmints have got to be hidin' out some-place,' Calvin replied. He looked up at the surrounding hills. 'The way I figure it, they've either got some nest up in those ranges, or they're operatin' from one of the ranches. Either way, I reckon it's time I had a look.'

'You want me to come along? I know the terrain.'

Calvin looked at him. 'You're deputy marshal now,' he said. 'I'll be needin' you to cover while I'm out of town.'

Hurlock glanced down at the silver star newly pinned to his chest and grinned.

'Whatever you say, Marshal,' he replied. 'You can depend on me.'

George Taber drew his gig to a stop beside a stream and jumped down in order to stretch his legs and let the horse take a drink. Although the sun had begun its descent, the air shimmered in the heat over the flatlands and gave the hills an unreal appearance. So far that day he had visited several small ranches and farms, but without success. In spite of his blandishments, nobody was much interested in taking out insurance. Still, his reception had been generally friendly. After all, he reflected, he was new to the district. It would take time for people to get to know him and for him to build up a clientele. A couple of people had expressed some interest and said they would think about it.

When the horse had finished drinking, he climbed back into the driver's seat and carried on his way. He had a rough idea of the area, but it still came as something of a surprise when he eventually reached a sign reading simply *Sycamore* and pointing to a rough track that led off from the trail he was following.

'*The Sycamore*,' he said, partly to himself and partly to the horse. 'Now ain't that the place Miss Jowett was makin' for?'

He spent a few moments in thought, removing his hat and running his hand through his hair as he did so. The place wasn't on his schedule, but he decided to pay it a visit. It was only a slight detour and who knew when he would be back that way? Flicking his whip over the head of the horse, he turned the gig into the new trail. It was headed in the direction of the hills and the horse slowed as the land gradually began to rise. After a time he came across cattle standing singly or in small groups scattered across the range and as he crested a rise he saw the ranch house in the middle distance. He pulled the gig to a halt to take in the scene. The ranch house was pleasantly situated with a grove of trees behind it and some corrals. At a little distance to the right stood another low building which Taber guessed was the bunk-house. Pulling on the reins, he moved forward again and had soon covered the distance between him and the ranch. He rode into the yard and as he drew to a halt the door of the ranch house opened and a woman emerged.

'Mr Taber,' she said, 'I thought I recognized you.'

'Miss Jowett. It's good to see you again.'

Behind her, a lace curtain twitched and he saw a face in the window. After a moment it vanished and then two figures appeared in the doorway: a boy and a girl of about ten and twelve. She glanced behind her.

'Get back,' she admonished. 'You seem to have forgotten your manners.' With a last look at Taber, they went inside. A man approached them from the direction of the bunkhouse.

'Cooper, can you take charge of Mr Taber's horse and buggy?' she said.

'Yes, ma'am.'

'Come on in,' she said to Taber. 'I have some coffee just on the boil.'

Taber climbed the steps to the porch and entered. His glance took in the room, which was simply but comfortably furnished. Miss Jowett directed him to a seat and then, excusing herself, went into the kitchen, returning quickly with a pot of coffee and two cups. He looked about for the children, but they weren't there.

'Ricky and Cora have gone to their rooms,' Miss Jowett said.

'They seem like nice kids.'

She smiled. 'Yes, they are. I shall have to introduce them before you go.' She poured the coffee and passed him a cup before taking a seat on a chair opposite him.

'Well,' she said, 'this is an unexpected surprise.'

'It is for me too. I happened to be passing by when I saw the sign to the Sycamore. On business, you understand.'

'Insurance? My brother might be interested, but I'm afraid he's not here just at the moment. As a matter of fact, he's gone to town on business himself.'

'No matter. It's nice to be here talking with you. Have you settled in?'

She looked down for a moment. 'It's lovely here,' she said, 'but I must admit it's taken me a while to get over the shock of what happened to the stagecoach.'

'That's hardly surprising,' he replied. 'It's just a great pity that you had to experience something like that.'

'Anyway,' she continued, 'how are you? You don't

seem to have wasted any time in getting on with your selling.'

'I'm used to moving about,' he said. 'The Armitas Company expects its representatives to be flexible.'

'You have no family ties, then?' she queried.

'No, ma'am. Like they say, wherever I hang my hat. . . .' He didn't finish the sentence, but instead took a sip of coffee.

'Have you seen anything of Mr Calvin?' she asked.

'No, but he too appears to be getting on with the job. The job of town marshal, I mean. For example, posters have appeared all over telling folks that the carrying of guns is banned.'

'A good thing too, I should say.'

They continued to talk in a desultory manner, and from time to time Taber could hear sounds from upstairs indicating the presence of the youngsters. He had drunk his second cup of coffee and was about to get to his feet when Miss Jowett suddenly turned to him with an anxious expression.

'Mr Taber,' she said, 'be careful.'

Her words took him by surprise. 'How do you mean?' he replied.

'I don't know. It's just that . . .' She hesitated. 'I can tell that my brother is worried. Yesterday, two strange men came to see him. I'm not sure – there was just something about them. They weren't like the other ranch-hands. My brother seems to be behaving normally, but I can tell that something's not right. It's not anything I can lay hold of, but it's there all the same. And after what happened . . .'

She broke off and Taber stood for a moment unsure what to say. Fortunately, at that moment there was a noise on the stair and the children appeared. Miss Taber looked up as they reached the bottom.

'You've timed that right,' she said. 'Mr Taber was just about to go, but I'd like you to meet him before he does. Mr Taber, this is Ricky and this is Cora. Children, say "hello" to Mr Taber.'

Taber took the hand of each in turn. 'Glad to meet you,' he said. 'I hope you're being good for your aunty.' He wasn't sure of the exact relationship between them, but the word 'aunty' seemed to go down perfectly well with all of them. They turned to her.

'We are good, aren't we?' the girl said.

'I already said as much to Mr Taber,' she replied.

The boy turned to him. 'Will you be coming back to see us?' he asked. Taber felt a little awkward. He wasn't used to dealing with youngsters.

'You will come and see us again?' Miss Jowett prompted, picking up on the boy's words.

'Yes, I'd like that,' he replied. He wasn't clear whether she meant in his capacity as insurance salesman or as an acquaintance. Without further ado, he made for the door. The gig was standing in the yard where he had left it and he mounted to the seat.

'Thank you for the hospitality,' he said.

Miss Jowett looked up at him. 'I'll tell my brother you were here. And I'll mention about the insurance. Wave goodbye, children.'

Taber hauled on the reins and the gig moved slowly away. He looked back as he left the yard. Miss Jowett and the children were standing on the veranda waving. He waved back and the next time he looked, they had gone.

Hurlock was feeling good. Just that morning the marshal had ridden off to take a look at the hills, leaving him in charge, and he was enjoying his sudden elevation and change of status. For a long time now he had been an insignificant figure around town, a figure of fun and the butt of jokes. Now, sitting in the Garter Saloon, enjoying a drink with a couple of the regulars, he could sense a definite change in their attitude.

'Yup, siree,' he was saying, 'the marshal told me he'd been lookin' for the right man for the job.'

'He ain't been in the job himself for more than a week,' one of his listeners replied.

'I guess he knew in advance the kind of man he wanted,' Hurlock replied.

'Yeah, you got the right credentials.' The two men laughed and Hurlock himself joined in.

'Go on, old feller. Have another.'

The man leaned over and poured a drink. Hurlock took the glass and took a hefty swig. He felt mellow and the world was a warm place.

'Here,' the other man said. 'Let me take a good look at that star.'

Hurlock thrust out his chest and the man pretended to examine the badge closely before finally breathing on it.

'Don't want to tarnish it,' he quipped.

The other man glanced across the bar-room. 'Say,' he said, 'Seems to me like there's someone over there packin' a pistol. Now ain't that banned? Maybe you should go over and do somethin' about it.'

Hurlock glanced in the direction the man indicated. His eyes seemed a mite blurry and the room heaved slightly.

'I don't see anybody carryin' a gun,' he said. He glanced down at his own thigh. 'Exceptin' me, that is.'

'And you're the deputy marshal. Over there – look. Go get him.'

Hurlock attempted to gather his senses. The man was right. Someone was carrying a six-gun. 'OK,' he said. 'I'll be right back.'

Getting awkwardly to his feet, he started to move towards the bar. He was not finding it easy to keep to a straight line, but almost to his own surprise, he found himself standing next to the man at the counter. He was a youngster, he could tell that much, and he was talking with one of the girls as the oldster tapped him on the arm. Breaking off the conversation, he turned and looked round.

'Haven't you seen the notice?' Hurlock managed to say.

'What notice?'

'New ordinance. No guns. Not in public. Afraid I'll have to ask you to turn in that shooter you're carryin'.'

The man hesitated for only a moment, then he reached into his holster and brought out the gun. He held it by the barrel as he handed it butt foremost to Hurlock.

'Sorry, marshal,' he said. 'I guess I just never saw any notice.'

Hurlock took the gun and after deliberating for a

moment, thrust it through his trouser belt.

'How do I get it back?' the youngster said.

'Call by the marshal's office any time. Don't worry. I'll be keepin' an eye on it.'

Hurlock turned and stumbled. He recovered his balance and began to walk back to the table where he had left his two companions. He had reached half-way when the sound of gunfire shattered the calm. Some of the girls began to scream while the men leaped to their feet. Hurlock had no idea what had happened. There was a lot of noise and confusion around him and the thud of boots on the floor. He felt himself being carried along as people rushed to the batwing doors. The air outside served to restore his senses and he saw a pall of smoke billowing down the street. People were running and shouting. A voice rang out:

'It's the Territorial Bank. Somebody's blown the safe!'

Suddenly reminded of his role as deputy marshal, Hurlock began to run towards the bank building, drawing his gun as he did so. Behind the screen of smoke, flame was spiralling into the air. Sparks flew and drifted overhead. He was running as fast as his ageing legs would carry him, trying to make sense of what was happening. Through the smoke a group of horsemen appeared, riding down on him. He heard gunshots and something whistled by his head. Shots were being fired from further along the boardwalk. The riders had spread out across the street and he flung himself sideways as the first horse brushed by. He hit the ground hard but managed to roll away, just avoiding the flying hoofs of another horse. One of the riders was yelling and whooping and the rattle of gunshots rang out loudly. He got to his feet as another riderless horse came by at a pace slow enough for him to be able to place a foot in the stirrup and swing himself aboard. Spurring it forward, he set off in pursuit of the riders. They had a good start on him and they were moving fast, but for a time he managed to keep them in his sights. One of the riders turned and began shooting at him. As they neared a junction, the riders split up, two of them veering off in another direction. Ignoring them, he plummeted on after the others. He was scarcely aware of what he was doing but he carried on the pursuit till they neared the edge of town, when suddenly his horse reared and he was thrown to the ground. He fell heavily and it took him a minute or so to get his wind and struggle to his feet. By the time he had done so the riders had gone, leaving nothing but a swirling cloud of dust in their wake.

He looked about. Back up Main Street a crowd had gathered. Flame and smoke continued to rise into the air. The horse had come to a halt a little way ahead and he walked over to it. A quick look convinced him that it was not hurt. A small group of people were running towards him and one of them shouted:

'Hurlock, are you OK?' They came up to him as he continued dusting himself down.

'You're too old for this!' he heard a voice say.

'Are you hurt? Someone get the doc!'

He shook his head, brushing away their concerns with a gesture of the hands. 'Don't worry about me,' he said. 'Just give me a chance to breathe.'

'Hell, you could have broken your neck taking off after them varmints like that.'

Somebody put his arm around Hurlock's shoulders. 'Help me get him back to the saloon,' he said.

'You done good, old feller.'

'He's wearin' a deputy's badge.'

Accompanied by the group, Hurlock began to walk back. From the comments that were being passed, he gathered that in general they were regarding him as something of a hero. He didn't feel that way himself, however. The only impression he had was that he had let the marshal down. The bank had

45

been robbed on his watch, and a lot of money had presumably been stolen. Calvin had trusted him to take care of things, and he had been more occupied with having a drink at the Garter Saloon than carrying out his duties. The crowd wanted to take him into the saloon, but he resisted and carried on walking. Smoke still billowed from the bank, but the flames had been doused. He stepped through the doors; inside, the place was a mess but the damage wasn't as bad as he expected. The walls were smoke-blackened and some of the windows had been blown out. The worst thing, however, was that one of the tellers was badly injured and two other men had been shot by the robbers making their escape. The bank manager stood nearby, coughing and wheezing.

'What happened?' Hurlock said.

'Isn't that obvious? Those varmints got away with a load of money.'

'They blew up the safe?'

'Yeah, and half the bank with it.'

'How much did it contain?'

'Everythin'.'

'Did you get a look at any of 'em?'

'Nope. They all had their neckerchiefs pulled up to mask their faces.'

Hurlock had other questions he wanted to ask, but

the bank manager was obviously in a state of distress so he decided to leave it and join the people who were continuing to dampen the smouldering areas of damage. The smoke was still quite thick and once it was apparent that the fire had been dealt with, everyone began to move. Hurlock made his way back up the street, assuring people that he was all right. When he reached the marshal's office, he staggered inside and slumped on a chair. He was feeling confused and riddled with guilt. What should he do next? Get a posse together? He glanced at the clock high on the wall. Time was getting along. It shouldn't be too long till the marshal got back. Maybe it would be better to leave it to him. He would know how to proceed. Placing his elbows on the table, Hurlock buried his head in his hands.

There could hardly have been a more marked contrast in mood as that between Hurlock and Gila with his bunch of desperadoes. The bank robbery had been a total success and they were in a frame of mind to celebrate deep in their valley hideout among the hills. Beer and whiskey were flowing freely; the only thing lacking was a supply of girls.

'It's OK for Gila,' one of the men was saying to Strawson, 'but what about the rest of us?'

Strawson slung back whiskey from the bottle he was holding. The amount he had drunk had given him courage. Getting to his feet, he stumbled over to where Gila stood at the entrance to his cabin. As he did so a number of shots rang out and he stopped for a moment to reach for his gun.

'Take it easy,' Gila said.

It only took a moment for him to realize, even in his bemused state, that it was only some of the boys letting off steam by firing into the air.

'Start gettin' trigger happy like that and it might not be good for your health.'

'What do you mean?'

'What do you think? I might get the impression you were thinkin' of usin' that gun on me.'

Strawson shook his head. He wasn't sure he knew what Gila was talking about. He needed to clear his thoughts. When he looked up, he saw the semi-naked form of the girl outlined in the lighted window behind Gila's head. It seemed to him she was beckoning him.

'The woman,' he mumbled.

Gila glanced over his shoulder and laughed. 'What about the woman?' he said.

'Need a woman. You've had your fun. You've finished with her. Share and share alike. Why not let somebody else have a turn.'

Gila's laughter ceased. He looked behind him again at the lighted window but the girl was gone. He turned back to Strawson.

'You like the girl?' he said. 'Well, that's natural. She sure knows how to please a man.'

Strawson swayed a little. The light from the window illuminated his coarse, leering features.

'Yes, sir, she sure knows what to do to make a man happy. Seems a shame, don't it, to keep it for myself. It's downright uncharitable not to let someone else enjoy her.' Strawson blinked but did not reply. Shouting and laughter rang on the air.

'Well, I can see how you might be feelin'. It ain't fair, is it? Nope, I can see how it might be. So why don't you go on in. Just think of her lyin' there, waitin' for you.'

Strawson licked his lips. For a moment he hesitated and then moved towards the door of the cabin. He reached for the handle and as he did so Gila's gun boomed three times. The bullets took Strawson in the back and he jerked and stiffened with the impact. As dark stains began to spread across his shirt, he turned his head to look at Gila with startled, uncomprehending eyes. He hung on to the door-frame for a few seconds, his face contorted with pain, till Gila's gun barked again and he finally slithered to the ground, blood now spurting from his chest. Gila moved slightly so that he stood over Strawson's twitching body and then emptied the rest of his gun into him. As his victim gave a final spasm, Gila refilled the chambers and put the gun back into its holster. After a moment the door flew open and Lottie appeared, almost stumbling over the corpse. She opened her mouth to scream, but Gila put a hand over her mouth and pulled her back inside.

'Get on the bed,' he hissed.

She looked at him with frightened eyes which only served to magnify his lust. Outside, there was a temporary lull in the festivities, but it was only a brief one. In a short time the din began afresh, serving to drown any sounds from inside the cabin.

Marshal Calvin sat with Hurlock on the balcony of his room overlooking the street, a bottle of whiskey on the table in front of them. Hurlock's glass was half empty and Calvin topped it up when he poured some into his own glass.

'Drink up,' he said. 'Ain't no use cryin' over spilt milk. What's done is done. It was my fault just as much as yours. No, in fact neither of us was to blame. Whoever carried out the bank job knew exactly what he was doin'.'

'Maybe so,' Hurlock replied.

'The thing to consider now is what we intend doin' about it.'

Hurlock reached out his arm and took a swig of the whiskey. 'What about you?' he said. 'You didn't come across anythin' suspicious?'

'No, but I learned a few things.'

'Yeah? Like what?'

'I called by a couple of ranches. Seems like they're losin' a lot of cattle. There have been a few incidents. Somethin' seems to be simmerin' under.'

'You're right there. I was talkin' with those two cowboys from the Sycamore when we rode out to meet the stage and they were sayin' the same thing. What do you reckon is goin' on?'

'Those cattle are bein' hidden someplace. Like I said before, maybe it's up in them hills or maybe one of the other ranchers is involved. Have you any idea who might be stirrin' things up, lookin' to take over some place maybe?'

Hurlock shook his head. 'Nope, but somebody's buyin' up a number of lots in town. That involves money.'

Calvin thought for a moment. 'Could be there's a connection. That money stolen from the bank would come in mighty useful for someone lookin' to make his mark.' He took another drink and when he spoke again it seemed to be about something else altogether.

'You've been around these parts for a long time,' he said. 'Tell me, have you ever come across the name Goad, Vin Goad?'

Hurlock thought for a moment before shaking his head. 'Can't say that I have,' he said. 'Why do you ask?'

'That varmint Wilton you recognized from the poster; he built up somethin' of a reputation, but he was only small time. He once rode for an outfit that was led by Goad. Now he was a different kettle of fish altogether. He was really mean and nasty, but he had some brains too. He had ambitions, and he might have gone a long way to achievin' them if he hadn't ended up in the penitentiary.'

Hurlock took another swig of the whiskey and a slow grin began to spread across his features.

'Now I'm wonderin' if this Goad *hombre* just happened to operate somewhere down Fromberg way.'

Calvin nodded. 'As a matter of fact, he did.'

'You put him in the pen,' Hurlock said. It wasn't a question but a statement.

'It's a long shot,' Calvin replied. 'But if Wilton was

around, it could be Goad is back on the owlhoot trail, too.' He took another drink before resuming.

'Whoever pulled off the bank job, it's a fair bet he's the one behind the stage robberies too. And the way I see it, he ain't goin' to be satisfied with that. Right now he'll be on a high and lookin' to cause more havoc. Trouble is, we just don't know for certain when or where he might decide to strike. Or he might just bide his time.' He paused before turning to the oldster.

'It's somethin' worth thinkin' about. Meanwhile, we'll see what luck we have with the posse. Personally, I don't think anything will come of it. Those outlaws ain't stupid enough to leave a trail takin' us right to their door. But some of the townsfolk are champin' at the bit and it'll give 'em somethin' to help burn off a little steam.' He glanced along the street. It was late and things were quiet.

'Reckon we might as well get some shuteye,' he concluded. 'We've got some ridin' to do tomorrow.'

The oldster downed the last of his glass before getting to his feet and walking down the stairs. Calvin watched as he emerged below and gave him a wave as he made his way to the next junction and disappeared. Then he went inside and lay down on his bed, thinking hard about what he had said. If there was anything in his theory about Vin Goad, he had a real fight on his hands: especially if Goad came to a similar realization that the new marshal of Medicine Bend was the same person who had put him behind bars once before.

CHAPTER THREE

As Calvin had anticipated, the posse's attempt to track the bank robbers came to nothing. They had followed the outlaws' tracks for a few miles out of town, but after that it was evident they had split up and gone their separate ways. The atmosphere was not good and a couple of the townsmen weren't averse to venting their feelings.

'You don't seem to have made much of an impression,' one of them said, accosting Calvin. 'We ain't had nothin' like this before. A few hotheads lettin' off steam around town is one thing, but this is somethin' else.'

'Hell, if we'd have known old Hurlock here was goin' to be left in charge, we'd have done somethin' about it ourselves,' another one added.

Calvin, who had been examining the ground, got to his feet. 'I'll find whoever robbed the bank,' he said. He glanced at Hurlock. The oldster was looking annoyed and was about to say something, but Calvin shook his head as a signal for him to be quiet.

'Yeah, sure! I wonder who'll be the next victim?' the man retorted.

Calvin didn't reply. He felt that his critics had a point. Things hadn't gone so well since he had taken over as marshal. It didn't matter that he had helped stem the stagecoach attacks and cleared weapons from the streets of the town; nor the fact that there wasn't really anything he could have done about the bank robbery.

'Let's get back,' he said.

He swung into the saddle and the posse started for town. Nobody spoke but there was a simmering sense of resentment. Hurlock rode close beside him.

'They ain't bein' fair,' he said.

'It doesn't matter. What does matter is catchin' those owlhoot varmints.'

'Sure thing. Three people got hurt. Next time it might be even worse.'

Calvin's features were grim. 'That's one more reason we've got to make sure there ain't a next time.'

56

The door of Brown's Eating House swung open and three men entered. The table nearest the window was occupied, but they didn't hesitate to make their way to it.

'Move!' one of them snapped.

'I beg your pardon? This table is occupied.'

'Was occupied. Now get up and move.'

'I'm sorry,' the man began, but he didn't get any further. Before he knew what was happening the newcomers had seized him by the collar and dragged him to his feet. One of them swung his fist and the man went reeling backwards, crashing into the table behind him. As he struggled to regain his equilibrium, another blow to the chin sent him to the floor. There he lay in a daze with blood pouring from his mouth where his teeth had bitten through his lip. On hearing the ruckus, Dolores had emerged from the back kitchen and watched with astonishment at the sudden unexpected eruption of violence. When she had recovered herself she rushed to help the hapless victim.

'Get out of my café!' she ordered the attackers.

The three men looked at each other and then burst into raucous laughter. 'Afraid we can't do that,' said the one who appeared to be their leader. 'In fact, you can get right back into your kitchen and make us some coffee.'

Dolores was on her knees, cradling the head of the injured man. She looked up with anger written across her features.

'Who do you think you are?' she gasped. 'What sort of people are you? Now I'll ask you once more to get out of my café before I go for the marshal.'

The men's laughter continued unabated. 'Hell,' one of them said, 'maybe we should just let her do that.'

'Shut up,' the leader snarled. 'You know what Gila's orders are, and they don't include gettin' involved with the marshal.'

'I was just sayin'. . . .'

'Look,' the leader said, addressing Dolores, 'if you don't want more trouble you'll do as I say. Now leave him alone and go make some coffee.'

Dolores looked at the injured man. His face was contorted in a grimace of pain, but he gave a faint nod. Gently laying his head down, she got to her feet and turned to face the man's attackers.

'I'm asking you to go,' she said. 'Have you no thought at all for anybody else?'

By way of reply the leader seized her and twisted

her arm sharply behind her back. 'I ain't tellin' you again,' he hissed. He jerked her arm upwards and she gave a whimper of pain. The response was more laughter as her assailant finally let her go. Burning with helpless indignation, she made her way across the café.

'Go and keep an eye on her,' the leader rapped, and one of the men followed her into the kitchen. The other two took their seats at the table from which they had ejected their victim and, pulling aside the curtain, looked out across the street at the marshal's office.

'You sure you'd recognize Calvin?' one of them asked.

'I ain't likely to forget. He put me and Gila and quite a few others behind bars.' The leader turned and spat on the floor. 'No, I ain't likely to forget.'

There was silence as they continued to observe the marshal's office. Presently, Dolores returned with her minder, carrying a tray on which were placed a jar of coffee and three cups.

'Pour!' the leader ordered.

Dolores glanced down at the injured man. 'He needs to see a doctor,' she said.

'You'll both need a doctor in a minute,' the leader replied.

Seeing that there was nothing else she could do, Dolores proceeded to pour the coffee. When she had finished the leader ordered her to sit at the next table. Then he turned his gaze back upon the street.

'What is it you want?' Dolores asked after a time.

The leader thought for a moment. 'This new marshal,' he replied. 'What did you say his name was?'

'I didn't say because I don't know.'

The leader got to his feet and before she could react he drew back his hand and hit her across the face.

'You're lyin',' he said. 'You know his name. Now what is it?'

'I tell you, I don't know his name. He's new in town.'

'He's called Calvin, ain't he?'

Dolores tried not to betray any sign that she recognized the name. She was spared further torment by the voice of one of the other hardcases.

'Quick! Somethin's happenin'.'

Quickly the leader drooped back into his seat and peered out the window. The door of the marshal's office had opened and the figure of Hurlock had appeared.

'Now what the hell is that joker doin' with a star on

his chest?' he asked.

Nobody had time to answer because, as Hurlock stepped out on to the boardwalk, a second figure appeared behind him. The men peered hard.

'That's him,' the leader said. 'That's Calvin.'

One of the others reached for his six-gun. 'Why don't we just shoot him right now?' he barked. The leader leaned forward and hit him hard on the arm. 'Don't be stupid!' he retorted. 'That ain't the way Goad wants to play it.'

The man admonished replied with a dirty look, but took his hand from the butt of his gun. 'What if he comes this way?' the other one said.

The leader had no need to reply because the marshal and his deputy turned and began to walk up the street in the opposite direction. When they had vanished from sight the man took a last swallow of the coffee and got to his feet. He looked at Dolores hard and then coming behind her, cupped his hands over her breasts. The other two looked on, their mouths twisted in an ugly leer.

'What do you say, boys?' the leader said. 'Maybe the lady would appreciate a little attention.'

'Get your hands off me, you scum,' Dolores hissed. She struggled to free herself but he only gripped her the harder. Dolores was desperately trying to think of what else she could do to escape when the man relaxed his grip and with a laugh turned and walked to the door.

'Don't think you can sleep easy,' he said, 'because we'll be back. You can count on that.'

Followed by his two henchmen, he clattered out of the door. Dolores sobbed and sank back in her chair. She was trembling and only vaguely registered the sound of galloping hoofs as the three outlaws eventually passed by, riding away out of town in the direction of the Sycamore ranch.

Taber sat alone at a table in a corner of the Garter saloon. The place was busy. Noise and smoke filled the air, which also smelled of stale liquor and damp sawdust. He wouldn't normally have spent any time there but he was feeling somewhat depressed. He thought a drink and some company might serve to buck him up, but if anything he was feeling worse. He had just about decided to leave when the batwings swung open and the burly figure of Ransome, the shotgun guard, came through. He glanced around and spotting the insurance man, to Taber's surprise came over to his table.

'Get you another?' he said, glancing at Taber's glass of whiskey.

'I'll buy,' Taber replied.

Ransome didn't offer any objections and as he took a seat, Taber made his way to the bar, returning with a bottle and an extra glass. He sat down and poured, topping up his own glass.

'How's it goin?' he asked.

'Not so good,' Ransome replied. 'You know the stage-line has closed? I don't know whether it's temporary or whether it'll open again. Until it does, that's me out of a job. How about you?'

'No one seems to be interested in takin' out insurance.'

'I ain't surprised. It isn't the kind of thing folks would spend much time thinkin' about. In fact, I don't understand it myself. But have you tried approachin' those prospectors up in the hills?'

'No. I've been mainly workin' the ranches.'

'You're not likely to do any better. It ain't like it is back East. Folk who come here lookin' to make a fortune diggin' in the earth or raisin' cattle ain't exactly the careful type.' There was a moment's silence before the former guard resumed the discussion.

'Just look what happened over at the bank,' he said.

Taber wasn't sure what precisely he was driving at.

'All the more reason why people should be thinkin' about lookin' for cover,' he replied. 'Financially, I mean.'

'There ain't no cover against the wrath to come,' Ransome replied.

Again, Taber wasn't sure how to take his remark, so this time he let it drop. Ransome took a swig of whiskey before fixing his gaze on Taber.

'Like I said, the stagecoach ain't runnin,' he said incongruously. 'I guess it's not surprisin', after those hold-ups and all. Maybe if they could get some folk willin' to volunteer as drivers and guards, they'd get the whole thing started up again. It's a real shame.'

'It's a pity,' Taber acquiesced.

'Guess it would take a lot of insurance,' Ransome said. 'Still, maybe it's somethin' the stage company might be interested in.'

Taber thought he saw the direction in which Ransome's thoughts were moving. 'You're right,' he said. 'I should be concentratin' my efforts on some of the businesses right here in town.'

'Maybe so, but I don't figure you'd do any better,' Ransome concluded. Taber looked at him, but the guard's face was giving nothing away.

'I don't suppose . . .' Taber began, thinking about Ransome's comments.

'Insurance? Count me out,' Ransome butt in. He paused for a moment before adding: 'Maybe you should be takin' out some insurance yourself.' Taber looked at him.

'For the horse and buggy, I mean,' Ransome added. 'Apart from anythin' else, you've been coverin' a lot of ground.'

'Oh, I see what you mean. Sure appreciate havin' the use of that old horse and buggy.'

'You'd get around a lot quicker if you forgot the buggy,' Ransome remarked. 'But maybe not if you're goin' to be stayin' in town.'

Taber felt a little wrong-footed. There seemed to be more to Ransome's comments than was at first apparent. Or perhaps he was just tired. He reached for his glass and downed the remainder of its contents.

'I think I'll be makin' tracks,' he said.

'There's still some whiskey in the bottle.'

'Help yourself,' Taber replied, 'you're welcome to it.'

He got to his feet, somewhat unsteadily. He realised he had drunk a little too much as he picked his way to the batwing doors and stepped outside. The cool night air struck him like a douche of water. He stood for a few moments looking up and down

Main Street. A lot of people were still round and light spilled from the stores which continued to trade. For no reason, he suddenly felt lonely as he bent his steps towards the room he rented on one of the cross streets. It wasn't far from the Mining Exchange building and as he passed he stopped and spent a few moments in thought. Then he continued on his way.

When Calvin heard about what had happened to Dolores, he was angrier than he would have expected. It was the doc who let him know, and Calvin didn't waste any time making for the eating house. When he entered, the place was as normal. A few people occupied the tables and Dolores was her usual self.

'I heard about what happened,' he said. She didn't reply and he sat down.

'Coffee?' she asked.

He nodded and she walked away. An elderly couple got to their feet and left. The only other customer was a man whom Calvin recognized as a member of the posse. Neither spoke and in a few moments Dolores returned. She set the coffee on the table and then glanced at Calvin.

'I'll put the sign up,' she said.

She went to the door and turned the card so it

read 'Closed'. Presently the remaining customer stood up and moved to the till where he paid. Dolores accompanied him to the door, let him out and then closed the door behind him. She stood for a moment before returning to the marshal's table where she sat down.

'So the news is around town,' she said.

'I don't know about that,' he replied. 'Doc Smith said there'd been some trouble. A man got beaten and . . .'

'Did the doctor say how he was?'

'He's fine. A few cuts and bruises and he was a bit groggy for awhile, but nothin' too serious.'

'It wasn't very nice,' she replied. Her voice was a little unsteady and for a moment he thought he detected her lip quiver. If so, she quickly pulled herself together. Without looking at him, she went on to describe what had happened, without dwelling too much on her role in the affair. Calvin didn't need all the details to be able to read between the lines.

'Could you describe any of the men?' he said.

Dolores shrugged. 'There was nothing special about any of them. They all looked mean. Apart from that, they could have been anybody.'

'No distinguishing features?'

She thought for a moment. 'No, I can't think of

anything. But I'd recognize them again if I saw them.'

'You hadn't seen any of them before?'

'No. I think I'd have remembered if I had.'

'If you don't mind, I'll maybe get you to look through some old Wanted dodgers.'

'There was something,' she said. 'I don't know whether it's relevant or not.'

He looked up at her. 'Yes,' he prompted. 'What was that?'

'The man who seemed to be their leader mentioned a name. Goad, I think it was.'

Calvin was suddenly alert. 'Goad,' he said. 'Are you sure it was Goad?'

'Yes, and one of them mentioned another name. It was an odd one. Let me think. Gila – that was it.' She couldn't mistake the keen look in his eyes.

'Are you quite sure about this?'

'Yes. I have a good memory for names – especially in circumstances like that. I might be wrong about Gila, but I'm definitely right about Goad.'

'That's really useful information,' Calvin prevaricated. He didn't want to give anything away by the tone of his voice, but it was clear to Dolores that the names meant something to him.

'You seemed to show interest when I mentioned

Goad,' she said. 'Do you know him?'

'It sounds familiar,' he replied, 'but there's probably nothin' in it.'

Dolores glanced at the diminishing amount of coffee in his cup. 'Can I get you some more?' she asked.

'Isn't the café shut now?' he replied.

'For other customers. Not for you.'

They exchanged glances and then she quickly got to her feet and walked across to the kitchen. She reappeared after a few minutes with a fresh pot and another cup.

'You don't mind me sitting beside you again?' she said. 'Seems like it's getting to be a habit.' She smiled faintly and he felt momentarily confused, but as she poured the coffee he quickly recovered himself.

'After this,' he said, 'we could maybe cross over to my office and take a look at those Wanted posters.'

'That sounds like a sensible idea,' she replied. She took a sip of coffee and then suddenly looked up at him.

'Oh,' she said, 'there's something else I didn't mention. Those three men seemed to know your name. In fact, they asked me if you were called Calvin.'

He took a long drink of the black coffee. 'What

did you tell them?' he asked.

'I didn't say anything, because it was just at that point they saw you through the window.'

Calvin's question was superfluous. If he had any doubts previously about Goad being the leader of the outlaw gang, he had none now. And it couldn't be an accident that the hardcases had mentioned his name. Goad must now know his identity just as he knew Goad's. There was no way of avoiding a confrontation. It looked like the scene was being set for a duel: a duel to the death for either or both of them.

The morning after his conversation with Ransome, Taber was woken by the sound of wheels passing in the street and the clopping of horses' hoofs. Sunlight streamed through the partially open curtains and shone on the wall. He lay still for a while, enjoying a feeling of well-being, before finally casting aside the sheet with a flourish and getting out of bed with a spring. His head was clear and he felt purposeful. Something had happened while he slept, as if an obstacle had been removed, as though he had been healed of some impediment. He felt physically lighter and he began to whistle as he performed his morning ablutions.

Bacon, eggs and strong black coffee, he reflected, *and*

then down to the General Store.

Without conscious thought, his brain had made a decision. He simply had to accept it. He glanced at his well-cut suit hanging in the wardrobe and shook his head. Ignoring it, he dragged his bag from under the bed and pulled out a shirt and a pair of jeans; they would do for the time being. He thought for a moment about what the ostler had said about the stage-line closing down. They needed drivers and guards; what was to stop him from volunteering?

He finished dressing and made for the door where he paused for a moment before going out. If he was taken on as a shotgun guard, he would need a rifle. Maybe the stage-line would provide it. What if they didn't accept him? What sort of credentials would they expect? He hadn't always worked as an insurance agent, and apart from anything else there was the experience he had gained during the Civil War. What if the Company had decided to wind things up altogether and were about to go out of business? As he stepped outside, a slow smile spread across his features. Already he was bringing up so many questions when the thing to do was to act. That questioning was the legacy of his days as a salesman. The thought even crossed his mind that it would be sensible not to hand in his notice till he had definitely landed

71

something else: as a kind of insurance, he mused. Then he almost laughed out loud. Hell, in any event there were other jobs.

It was then that he made his decision. He wouldn't volunteer to be a driver or a guard. Instead, he would try his hand at prospecting. Plenty of people did it. Some of them even struck lucky. He looked up and down the street. A few children were playing with a hoop. Ladies in gingham dresses and bonnets were making their way towards the centre of town. A man on horseback passed in the opposite direction. A dog ambled along and stopped to cock its leg against a neighbouring fence. Birds sang and the sun shone out of a blue sky. Feeling invigorated, he stepped out briskly.

Hurlock returned to the marshal's office after having done the rounds of the saloons, collecting a number of weapons for safe storage in the process. Calvin himself was in a meeting with some of the local citizens to discuss town affairs. Hurlock had chuckled when the marshal told him about it because he guessed that Calvin would hate this aspect of his role. He placed the weapons in a bureau and then sat down at the desk. It was pleasant to be out of the heat and his eyes were beginning to close when he was roused to attention by a knock on the door.

'Come on in!' he yelled.

The door opened and a stranger entered. Something about him put Hurlock on the alert. The man glanced around.

'Where's the marshal?' he said.

'He ain't here. I'm the deputy marshal. If you've got somethin' to say, you can say it to me.'

The man looked hesitant and uneasy. His eyes were shifty and they flickered like those of a lizard. He licked his lips.

'I'd rather see the marshal,' he said.

'He won't be around for a while.'

The man seemed to be struggling with himself. 'Can you give him a message?' he asked.

'Sure. But it might be easier if you just told me what's on your mind.'

The man thought for a moment and Hurlock wondered if he was about to unburden himself. He turned towards the window and peered outside before replying.

'Tell him to meet me at Wickeyup Wash,' he said. 'You know the place?'

'Sure.'

'Make certain you tell him.' The stranger turned and made for the door.

'What time would that be?'

'Sundown.'

'That ain't exactly precise.'

'Just tell him. I'll be there.'

Before Hurlock could say anything else, the man opened the door and was gone. Hurlock got to his feet with the intention of following him, but then thought better of it. Whatever the man wanted, it was obvious it was only Calvin he would deal with. It was also pretty apparent to Hurlock that the man was not one of the town's regular citizens. In fact, he looked more like a member of the gun-slinging fraternity. If that was the case, he could be setting a trap for the marshal. On the other hand, if Calvin had been there, the man would have had no need to suggest a rendezvous. Either way, Calvin would need to be extremely careful and, if necessary, he intended going along as back-up.

Miss Jowett stood on the veranda of the ranch house, looking out for Ricky and Cora, who had gone riding. They were both quite accomplished riders so she didn't feel too concerned, but they had been gone longer than she expected. She was watching a wide sweep of rangeland when a horseman appeared. It wasn't either of the youngsters and for a few moments, till he got closer, she did not realize that it was her nephew. As he rode into the yard and swung down from the saddle, one of the ranch-hands appeared and took his horse.

'Candia,' he said. 'Is everythin' OK?'

'Yes. I was just admiring the view. You know, you have a really nice place here.'

He mounted the steps to the veranda and stood beside her. 'Yes, it sure is,' he replied. He put his arm around her shoulder and gave her a hug. 'You know, it's good to have you around. You help me appreciate what I've got. Since Rebecca died . . . well, it's been a while now, but I guess I've only just started to get used to bein' without her. And the kids sure appreciate havin' you around.'

They stood for a while in silence till he spoke again. 'By the way, where are the children?'

'They've gone for a ride. They should be back any time. I only wish I was a better rider and I could go with them.'

'I'm sure they'd like that, but they've been around horses long enough to know how to take care of themselves.' He paused and when she looked up at him he seemed thoughtful.

'Is there something else?' she asked.

He gave her a gentle squeeze and then smiled. 'I

guess you know me pretty well,' he said. 'As a matter of fact, there is somethin'. I've been meanin' to talk to you but with one thing and another – you know how it is.'

'Go on,' she replied.

'I don't know how to put it. Maybe it's nothin'.'

'Since I've been here, I couldn't help but notice that there seems to be something in the air.'

'You know I had a meeting in town with a few of the other ranchers. It seems we've all been losin' some stock. To rustlers, I mean. That maybe wouldn't matter too much – some losses are to be expected. But it's the scale of it that's worryin'. It's been gettin' worse and there have been one or two other incidents.'

'What sort of incidents?'

'Nothin' much; a few unknown riders trespassin' on private range, one of the streams providin' water bein' blocked up; a few threats. None of it taken alone amounts to much, but they're all straws in the wind.'

'Do you think somebody is behind it?'

'I don't know. But look what happened to you and that stagecoach. And then there was the bank robbery in town. Could be it's all part of a pattern.'

'What do you mean, a pattern?'

'Maybe someone's lookin' to drive us out.' He looked up towards the distant hills. 'It seems to me like there's more than a bunch of prospectors workin' those peaks. Looks as though there might be a regular outlaw roost up there.'

'I knew you were worried.'

He squeezed her once again. 'I don't want you to be concerned,' he replied. 'Maybe I'm exaggeratin'. There's probably nothin' to it.'

'I'm glad you told me,' she said. She looked out across the sweep of rangeland and, seeing two riders in the distance, felt a sudden release of tension.

'Here come Ricky and Cora,' she said.

CHAPTER FOUR

Calvin and Hurlock approached Wickeyup Wash, a shallow pool surrounded by a grove of trees, just as the sun dipped below the western horizon.

'I don't like this,' Hurlock remarked. 'We could be ridin' straight into a trap.'

'I don't think so,' Calvin replied, 'but just in case, we'll leave our horses here and I'll go the rest of the way on foot.'

'What do you mean, *you'll* go the rest of the way?'

'Think about it. If he sees the both of us approachin', our man might start gettin' nervous.'

'He'd recognize me.'

'Maybe so, but he might still be deterred. You wait here and watch the horses.' They dismounted and Calvin drew his gun from its holster.

'Be careful,' Hurlock said. 'If there's any trouble, I'll come right on in.'

Calvin nodded and began to move stealthily forwards. As he got near the Wash, the slanting rays of the sun were broken into dancing patches of light and shade by the branches of the trees; the breeze made the leaves rattle. Suddenly he tensed. Some obstacle lay across the path a little way ahead of him. He crouched, ready to respond to any sign of movement, but the object remained immobile. Still he waited till he was satisfied that whatever it was, it held no threat, and then he started inching forwards again. He could see now that it was the body of a man, lying face down, partially in and partly out of the water. When he was beside it, he kneeled down and turned it over. The man had been shot in the chest and was quite obviously dead. Standing upright, he dragged the corpse clear of the water and then spent a few moments in thought. It seemed the man had been genuine and Hurlock's worries about a trap were unfounded. But what had he been up to? Why had he arranged to meet him here at the Wash and who had killed him? He was still turning the matter over when he heard footsteps behind him and turned quickly, gun in hand, to see Hurlock coming towards him.

'Damnit, you should be more careful,' he rasped. 'I coulda shot you.'

'You've been a long time. I was gettin' worried.' Hurlock glanced down at the body on the ground.

'Looks like we'll never know what his game was,' Calvin remarked.

Hurlock leaned over the corpse, looking at it closely. 'That ain't the man who came to see me,' he said.

'What? It's not him?'

'Nope. That isn't the same man.'

Calvin looked at the corpse. 'Then who the hell is he?' he said.

Hurlock glanced about. Darkness was descending and he was clearly nervous.

'Come on,' Calvin said, sheathing his six-gun. 'Let's get back.'

He turned and began to walk away, closely followed by the oldster. Neither of them spoke and Calvin's mind was preoccupied with his thoughts. It wasn't far to where they had left the horses and it was only when they had almost reached them that a man stepped out of the shadows with a rifle in his hands pointed straight at the marshal. Calvin cursed beneath his breath. He had been careless and the man had the drop on them. Then, just behind him, he heard a gasp from Hurlock who muttered: 'That's him. That's the man.'

Calvin peered closely at the figure confronting him. The man's rifle had dropped a little and then he spoke.

'Sorry about the reception, but I had to be sure it was you.'

'I'm Calvin, Marshal of Medicine Bend. And this is my deputy, Hurlock.'

'I know about the deputy. We've already met.'

'And who are you?'

'The name's Snell. Not that it matters.'

'Well, now the introductions have been made, maybe you could put that rifle down and tell us just what exactly is goin' on.'

The man hesitated a moment longer before lowering the rifle.

'Go on,' Calvin said. 'You told Hurlock you wanted to see me. You set up this meetin'. Well, here I am. If you've got somethin' to say, go on and say it.'

The man looked from Calvin to Hurlock. 'You found the body?' he said.

'Yes. Did you kill him?'

The man didn't reply. Calvin, peering through the gloom, thought he might have seen the man's head nod as if in agreement. When he spoke again, it was on a different theme.

'Is there a reward out on that bank robbery? I mean, if someone had some information it ought to be worth somethin'.'

'Is that what you wanted to see me about?'

'Look, I got to think about myself, what I get out of all this.'

'You're not makin' a lot of sense. If you've got somethin' to say about the bank job, you could have told my deputy.'

'It ain't just the bank job. That's only part of it.'

'Part of what?'

The man was clearly agitated. 'Look,' he said, 'if I tell you what I know, you've got to promise to give me somethin' in return.'

'That all depends on what information you claim to have.'

'I got plenty, and it's all true.'

'Go ahead then. I'm listenin'.'

The man wiped a hand across his mouth and then spat. After a few moments' thought he seemed to come to a decision.

'Look,' he said, 'I know who carried out the bank job.'

'I've got a pretty good idea myself. You're gonna have to do better than that.'

'How would you know?'

Calvin gave a gentle laugh. 'Let me make it easy for you,' he said. 'The person behind the bank robbery and the stage hold-ups is a man called Vin Goad.'

He had put the name out at a venture but Snell's response was unmistakable. He made no effort to conceal his surprise.

'How do you know his name?' he said, repeating himself.

'I know quite a lot more. For example, it's my guess you're a member of his gang.'

The man was visibly shaken. 'I had no part in the bank job,' he blurted out. 'In fact, I don't want any part of what Goad is up to. The man is mad. You know they call him *Gila*. That's because he keeps a Gila lizard as a pet. No, not a pet; he treats it like it was his best friend. That's probably because he ain't got any other friends. He don't mix with any of the boys. He's got a woman, but what he really likes to do is get away by himself and spend his time in a cave talkin' to that lizard. He's deranged. And he treats people as if they were the reptiles. I don't claim to be any kinda saint, but he's evil.'

'Is that a general comment or have you got a more personal reason for feelin' that way?'

'I got plenty of reasons. Strawson was my friend. Me and him, we rode together a long time. Gila didn't give him a chance.'

'Who's Strawson?'

'It doesn't matter. He's dead now, shot down in cold blood.'

'Is that what happened back there?' Calvin said, with a jerk of his thumb over his shoulder.

'He had a fair chance. It was his own fault. He must have seen me comin' out of the marshal's office in town. He must have followed me to Wickeyup Wash. Anyway, he got the jump on me, but I got the better of him. Like I said, it was either him or me. I doubt whether Gila will even notice he ain't around any more, but all the same there's no way now I can go back. You've got to help me get away from Gila.'

'You haven't told me anything so far that I didn't already know.'

Snell was getting more agitated. He was being out-manoeuvred but suddenly he seemed to have an idea.

'There's one thing I can tell you that you don't know.'

'What's that?' Calvin said.

'I know where Goad is hiding out. I could take you there.'

It was Calvin's turn to be thoughtful. Clearly, if the town and the territory were to achieve peace, Goad and his gang needed to be dealt with. There might be ways of drawing him out or tracking him down, but they were likely to be time consuming and all the while Goad would be a constant menace. Weighing up the situation, he came to a decision.

'OK,' he said. 'Now I might be interested.'

'I'll show you, but I'll need somethin' in return.'

'The only thing you'll get in return might be a pardon if Goad is brought to justice and you're prepared to give evidence against him.'

'No deal,' the man said. 'I ain't goin' near any court. Like I said, I had nothin' to do with that bank job.'

'And what about the stagecoach robberies? I suppose you had no part in them either?'

'Look, I've gone out of my way already to help you. I could have just rode away and not told anybody about Goad.'

'There's nothin' to stop you doin' that. Go right ahead.' The man didn't say anything in reply.

'I know somethin' about how Goad operates,' Calvin said, 'and from what you've told me, so do you. He ain't the type to let anyone escape his clutches. Am I right? The only way you can be sure that Goad won't catch up with you is if he's behind bars.'

'He wouldn't know anythin'about all this?'

'Not unless I somehow let it slip that you'd been in touch. News like that is liable to spread pretty quickly.'

'You wouldn't do that,' Snell said.

'Try me,' Calvin replied.

Through the gloom, Calvin could see the man's eyes peering closely at him. 'I don't know,' he eventually said. 'I gotta think about this. I gotta go.'

'Sure,' Calvin said. 'You know where I am. Go away and think about it. I'll give you till noon the day after tomorrow.'

'That ain't long.'

'It's long enough,' Calvin said.

'I can't take the risk of bein' seen again in town.'

'You'll find a way.'

The man opened his mouth as if to say something more, but then turned on his heels and began to walk away in the direction of the Wash. In a few moments he had vanished among the trees.

'Was that wise? I mean lettin' him go like that,' Hurlock said.

'We got no reason to detain him. Besides, he'll be back.'

'I hope you're right,' Hurlock replied.

Calvin began to move towards the horses. 'Come on,' he said. 'I figure we've had enough excitement for one night. Let's head back to town.'

Vin Goad had plenty to think about. His men had come back from town with the information that the new marshal of Medicine Bend was indeed his old adversary, Wade Calvin. That was one thing. For years he had nursed the desire for vengeance and now it seemed the opportunity had fallen right into his lap. The second thing was how to go about acquiring the Sycamore ranch. He had been applying pressure for some time, but he was getting tired of all that now. He needed to carry out a decisive act. The proceeds from the bank robbery, taken together with the money he had acquired from holding up the stage-coach, had given him more then enough to go ahead and make an offer. But, quite apart from the fact that Jowett, the owner, would never accept a bid, that just wasn't the way he operated.

'What do you think?' he said, addressing the lizard which as usual was biting at his glove. 'Which one of the stinkin' coyotes do we deal with first? Calvin or Jowett?' He looked away, thinking, and then burst into a wild laugh.

'I think Calvin can wait,' he said. 'Don't you agree? We wouldn't want him to die too easily. Oh, no! That wouldn't be fair; not after everythin' he's done. No, Calvin needs to suffer. When he dies, it's goin' to be slow and painful.'

He laughed again, and this time it developed into a wild prolonged cackle that rang round the walls of the cave. The lizard's tongue flicked out and then it clamped its teeth into the leather glove where it hung on tenaciously as Goad shook his hand. Goad continued to laugh but then it stopped as suddenly as it had begun. He prized the Gila monster's jaws apart and slipped it back into a pocket. For a long time he sat in silence, gently rocking backwards and forwards, and contemplating the plan he had come up with for dealing with Jowett. It was strange he hadn't thought of it before. There were two kids living at the ranch. What could be easier or more obvious than to kidnap them? They would provide the best possible bargaining counters. Jowett would have no choice: the Sycamore ranch in exchange for their release.

Perfect. The ranch was as good as his. But he had no intention of releasing the captives.

Taber rode his mule up into the hills. He carried with

him a rifle and a six-shooter, together with some basic necessities and equipment. He was well aware of the dangers and difficulties that awaited him, and he was aware too of how slim were his chances of success. Nevertheless, the carefree feeling that had been with him when he awoke the morning following his discussion with Ransome still remained.

He was enjoying the country. He had entered a valley drained by a number of streams, their banks lined with cottonwood trees, and above him the green and purple peaks were outlined against a sky of blue. He had penetrated some way into the hills, past the more well-worked areas, but he knew he would need to go even further to have the remotest chance of spotting any traces of silver-bearing ore which hadn't yet been found. His eyes still searched the outcrops of rock for tell-tale black lines that might indicate what he was looking for. Occasionally he saw an isolated tent or a lone figure in the distance but it wasn't till late in the day, when he was thinking of making camp, that he came across a little group of men working one of the streams, labouring hard and dipping metal bowls into the sand and gravel of the river bed.

When he was still at a little distance, he stopped to watch them. It looked like back-breaking work.

Nearby, a rocker was in use to extract larger items from the water, and it was apparent to Taber that they were looking for gold rather than silver. Higher up, in a tributary stream, a small group was gathered round a series of connected wooden troughs along which the waters of the stream had been diverted by means of a wooden sluice. One man was shovelling dirt into the trough, others were stirring it up so that the finer sand sieved through and any gold was caught. The men were intent on the job and didn't seem to notice him, so after a short while he urged the mule forward and rode close. One of them stood up, stretching his back.

'Howdy,' he said.

'Howdy,' Taber replied. 'Are you havin' any luck?'

'Not much,' he replied. He took a few steps and Taber observed that he carried a limp. 'We'll be down to our last pot of coffee at this rate.'

Taber took only a moment to think. 'I've got some supplies. I figure I could spare a few items. You're welcome to have them.'

The man looked up at him quizzically. 'That's real nice of you,' he said.

Taber got down from the mule. One or two of the men glanced in his direction but in general they seemed incurious. Taber undid some of his packs.

'Go on,' he said. 'Take what you need.'

The man picked out a few items, including coffee. As he did so Taber asked him if he knew any of the miners that had struck it rich. The man laughed and then looked up towards the more distant peaks. In the late sunlight, they looked unreal.

'I figure if there's any real gold, it's likely to be up there.'

'Why are you workin' your claim here then?' Taber said.

The man glanced down at his leg. 'This is one reason why,' he said.

'How do you mean?'

'Go anywhere near those peaks and you're likely to end up dead. I got a little too close and I was lucky to come away in one piece. More or less.' Taber looked blank and the man continued:

'Somewhere up there is a gang of owlhoots. I figure they've made it their base. We've had some trouble down this far. That's why we banded together. If I were you, I wouldn't think of goin' much further.'

'I don't see why they would choose to pick on me,' Taber replied.

'They'll pick on anybody. And they don't have to have a reason.'

91

Taber began to fasten his packs again. 'Any idea who they are?' he asked. The man shrugged.

'Outlaws, drifters, hardcases and just about anyone looking for a fast grubstake. Mainly outlaws, I guess. The mountains are a good hideout.'

'Thanks for the warnin',' Taber said.

The man looked at him and smiled. 'Thanks for the supplies.' He stuck out his hand and Taber took it in his own. Then he got back on the mule.

'Be seein' you,' he said.

As he rode away he was deep in thought. Could these outlaws the man had told him about be the same ones who had carried out the attacks on the stagecoach and blown up the bank back in Medicine Bend? If so, their influence seemed to stretch a long way. He would need to take care. For one moment he thought of making his way back the way he had come but it was only for a moment. Suddenly he burst into a laugh. Where did his insurance schemes fit into this order of things? Maybe they had a place, maybe they were relevant, but as things stood at that moment they only seemed absurd.

Ricky and Cora rode their horses at an easy canter. It was a beautiful day and they were enjoying themselves. Presently they drew to a halt and Ricky came up close to his sister.

'We've come quite a way from the ranch house,' he said. 'Maybe we should be gettin' back.'

'There's plenty of time,' Cora said. 'I tell you what. I'll give you a race as far as the line shack on the east range.'

Ricky didn't spend much time thinking about his sister's challenge. 'You're on,' he said.

Instantly, she dug her spurs into her horse's flanks and the gelding broke forward. Ricky was only a few seconds behind and soon they were racing neck and neck, their horses' lips quivering and flecks of foam beginning to fly from their extended nostrils. It was exhilarating and Ricky couldn't help whooping with pleasure. They both rode excellent cutting horses, trained to accelerate quickly from a standing start. The wind blew into their faces and lumps of turf flew into the air. Ricky began to edge into the lead, but Cora quickly drew level again. Their attention was concentrated on the ride and neither noticed that a group of four horsemen had appeared on their right, approaching rapidly at an angle so as to cut them off. It wasn't till they heard the sharp crack of a rifle that they realized they were no longer alone. They turned their heads and, seeing the riders, slowed slightly while veering to their left.

'Who are they?' Cora shouted.

'Don't know. Must be some of the ranch-hands.'

'Why would they start shooting?'

They peered closer and it was soon apparent that the riders, whoever they were, did not belong to the Sycamore.

'Keep going!' Ricky shouted.

He was expecting further shots to be fired, but they didn't come. He concluded that the first shot was meant as some kind of warning, but if so it had the opposite effect. Instead of slowing down and stopping, they spurred their horses harder and for a while it seemed they were gaining an advantage. The group of riders began to fall behind, but their own horses were tiring. Suddenly Cora's gelding staggered as its hoof went into a hollow. She clung on and the horse seemed to have recovered its balance when it went over head first, flinging the girl to the ground. Subconsciously, she had partly prepared for it and she was quickly back on her feet again as the horse struggled to its feet. Ricky drew his own mount to a halt just as the riders arrived on the scene. One of them held a rifle and they were all mean looking. Ignoring the men, Cora ran up her horse. It was standing with its head hanging, panting and with steam rising in a cloud from its body, but it seemed to be uninjured. She turned to the man with the rifle.

'What do you think you're doing!' she snapped. 'My horse could have been killed.'

He grinned. 'I signalled for you to stop. It's your fault if you decided to carry on ridin' like that.'

'Who are you?' Ricky said. 'Don't you realize this is private property?' The man with the rifle turned to his companions and they all began to laugh.

'Now what are we gonna do?' one of them joked. 'Looks like we'll be arrested for trespass.'

The leader sheathed his rifle, dismounted and approached Cora. She took a step back as Ricky jumped down from his horse. He made to go to her but he didn't get far as a couple of the riders, following his example, got down and seized him by the arms.

'Let me go,' he said, struggling to free himself.

Cora was sobbing. As the leader of the group came up to her she struck out at him with her fists, but she was helpless to resist. As he grasped her around the waist, the others broke into laughter again. She still continued to struggle as her assailant lifted her from the ground and hoisted her back into the saddle.

'Take it easy, lady!' he hissed.

The two who had seized Ricky, pinioning his arms

behind his back, now dragged him to his horse and ordered him to get back on board.

'Who are you?' he repeated. 'Whoever you are, you won't get away with this.'

The men ignored him and swung themselves back into leather. They took the reins of his horse while the leader did the same with Cora's and then they started to ride.

'Where are you taking us? Cora shouted. 'Let us go!'

There was no reply from the men as their horses began to pick up speed. She looked across at her brother. He spread his hands and she took it as a signal of support. She looked about for any sign of her father's ranch-hands, but the range was empty. As Ricky had remarked, they had already come a long way from the ranch house before even starting on the race for the east range. They were near the limits of the Sycamore spread and seemed to be heading towards the hills. Suddenly, she felt very afraid.

It was late and Calvin was about ready to turn in for the night when he thought he heard a noise outside on the landing. Immediately, he drew his six-gun and stepped to the door where he listened intently, his ear pressed against the wood. He remained that way for some time, but the sound was not repeated. Standing to one side, he put his hand on the door-knob and, turning it, flung the door wide open. The passage outside was dark; only a faint gleam showed at the top of the stairs. Down below was his office and the cells, which at the moment held no prisoners. He was about to go back inside when he thought he heard it again, a soft sound like a footstep. He made to move towards the stairs when he stopped and instead went back into his room. Leaving the door open, he tip-toed to the balcony overlooking the street. He glanced up and down. The street was deserted but away along it he could see a horse teth-ered to a hitch-rack. Placing his gun carefully back in its holster, he climbed over the rail. It was quite a drop to the street below. Holding on to the rail, he lowered himself down as far as he could and then let go. He landed more heavily than he had intended and as he got to his feet the outer door to his office opened wide and a man came running out. Quick as he was to react to Calvin's presence, Calvin was just as quick and as the man ran past, he threw himself side-ways and brought him down in a heap. Calvin dragged him to his feet.

'Snell!' he breathed. His gun was back in his hand

and he held it close to the outlaw's face. 'You'd better have a good explanation for what you're doin' here.'

Snell was breathing heavily. 'It isn't like it might seem,' he said.

Calvin lowered his gun. 'Get inside!' he snapped.

Snell staggered up on to the boardwalk and into the marshal's office. Calvin came right behind, slamming the door shut after him. He pushed Snell into a chair.

'OK,' he said, 'start talkin'.'

'I came to see you,' Snell said.

'Funny way to go about payin' a visit.'

'You gave me till noon tomorrow. I didn't want anybody to see me. I figured if you weren't around, I could at least stay till the mornin'. Nobody would think of lookin' for me here. Really, I'm scared. Gila has a way of findin' out things. If he knew I'd been talkin' with you. . . .'

'How did you get in?'

'That's easy for somebody like me. I reckon you should get your locks changed.'

It was dark in the room; Calvin made to light the lamp but Snell put a hand on his arm to stop him.

'Somebody might see me,' he whimpered.

'Take it easy,' Calvin said. 'There ain't nobody around. Besides, the blinds are down.'

He lit the lamp but turned it low. Now he could make out the man's features more clearly, he was inclined to believe Snell's story. He was not making it up; he was clearly frightened and nervous. He moved to his desk and from one of the drawers produced a bottle of whiskey and a couple of tin mugs. He poured two drinks and gave the larger one to Snell.

'Try some of this,' he said. 'It might help to calm you down.' Snell took a swig. 'Thanks,' he said.

'You seem to go about things in a funny sort of way,' Calvin remarked.

'I don't like to be around town. Gila's got men here. It just ain't safe.'

Calvin took a sip of the whiskey. 'Do I take it from this little caper that you've made your mind up about Gila?'

The man wiped his mouth from which a trickle of whiskey had run. 'The way I see it, I ain't got no choice.'

'You're willin' to show us where Gila has his hideout?'

'I can tell you.'

'That ain't good enough. I need someone to show me the way right there.'

The man took another swig and began to sputter. 'If I do, you gotta make sure Gila don't get away.' By way of reply, Calvin broke into a chuckle.

'What are you laughin' at?' Snell said.

'Hell,' Calvin replied, 'how many men has he got up there? We'll be lucky if we come away alive ourselves.'

'How do you mean? You'll need to put a posse together.'

Calvin laughed again. 'Nope,' he said, 'that ain't the way I aim to do it. Besides, I'd never get enough men to volunteer.' Snell's puzzled expression changed to one of horrified disbelief.

'Don't worry,' Calvin said. 'Just show me where Goad is hidin' out, and leave the rest to me. You don't need to get involved more than that.' He leaned over and poured more whiskey into the outlaw's mug.

'Make yourself at home,' he said, and made for the stairs.

'Where are you goin?' Snell asked.

'Where do you think? This sort of thing might appeal to you. Me, I need some sleep. You can have the rest of that bottle.' He put one foot on the stair and then glanced back at Snell.

'Oh, and if it makes you feel any easier, you can turn off that lamp.'

CHAPTER FIVE

It wasn't the first time that the youngsters had stayed out later than she would have liked, but this time Miss Jowett was seriously concerned. The minutes ticked by and they were already an hour overdue. Each time she thought of doing something, she resolved to give them another five minutes. Finally, she could bear the tension no longer and came to a decision. She walked over to the bunkhouse and knocked on the door. After a few moments one of the ranch-hands appeared, a man she knew called Bassett.

'Hello, ma'am,' he said. He immediately saw the worried look on her face. 'Is somethin' wrong?' he asked.

'Maybe I'm being a foolish old woman, but I'm

worried about the children. They should have been back by now.'

'I wouldn't be too concerned,' he replied. 'They're both old enough to look after themselves.'

'All the same, I'd appreciate it if somebody could go and look for them.'

The man thought for a moment. 'I'll go,' he said. 'Have you any idea which direction they went?'

'I'm afraid not. They sometimes mention the east range, but they could have gone anywhere.'

He observed again the anxious look on her face. 'Don't worry,' he repeated. 'They won't have gone any further than the boundary of the Sycamore. I'll find them directly.'

'Thank you. I really appreciate it.'

The man quickly made his way towards the stables and a few minutes later Miss Jowett saw him ride away, accompanied by another of the ranch-hands. She felt slightly better but couldn't settle to anything. She walked up and down the veranda, occasionally stepping down and going as far as the fence. *Maybe they're with their father, she thought, or some of the other ranch-hands.* That sometimes happened, although in the case of their father it had usually been pre-arranged. She felt her helplessness. Really, she was out of her depth living on the ranch. She liked the place, and she got on well with her young charges. But the style of life remained somewhat alien to her. If only she could have ridden a horse as well as Cora and Ricky, she would have gone with them, but they probably wouldn't have wanted her to do so anyway. Maybe she had been remiss in not getting one of the cowboys to accompany them. Her nephew had never expressed any real concern and she didn't want to appear too much like an old mother hen. Besides, he had worries enough, and she wouldn't have wanted to bother him further.

After all, that was the reason she had come out West in the first place, to try and lighten him of his domestic burdens. She turned and went back into the house and made her way into the kitchen where she got out a moulding board and flour. There were other ways to try and kill time. She set about baking some warm biscuit. It would be nice to have later, with honey, when everyone returned to the ranch.

Early in the morning, before many people were about, Calvin and Hurlock, accompanied by Snell, rode out of Medicine Bend. Early as it was, Dolores Brown was up and about and she watched them from the doorway of her eating house till they turned a corner and were out of sight. She didn't know what they were up to, but she was shrewd and could guess. Calvin had more or less let it be known that there would no peace for the town till the outlaw threat was removed. The outlaws were up in the hills, and that's the way they were headed.

Calvin had given serious thought to the idea of forming a posse, but he had decided against it, partly for the reason he had given Snell. The fact of the matter was that he preferred to operate alone or in a tight partnership. He had ridden that way for most of his life; that was how he had done things back in Fromberg, the way he knew best. He also thought he knew how Goad's gang operated. If his previous experience was to be repeated, they would be likely to crumple once their leader was taken out. That was his plan; get Goad, then mop up his disoriented followers. It wasn't much, but he could be thinking about it on the way to Goad's hideout. He also figured it was wise to remain flexible; a lot would depend on circumstances and it was wise not to be too hidebound.

He glanced at the diminutive figure of Hurlock. The oldster wasn't perhaps the person he would have envisaged riding with, but he had proved himself. He realized that for some time before his arrival, Hurlock had been an object of amusement around town, but he had sensed his essential quality. All Hurlock had needed was someone to invest some faith in him. He felt confident that the oldster would not let him down. About Snell he was far less confident. The man was unreliable; for all they knew, his whole story could still be some elaborate plot to lead them into a trap. However, he didn't think so. As far as he could see, the man was genuinely afraid and looking for a way to escape from the mesh in which he had become embroiled. Most of all, he wanted to be rid of the ever present threat of Gila.

Their route took them past the stagecoach depot. Two Concord coaches stood in the yard and behind them was a corral with a number of horses. The depot was closed but there was a man sitting on a bench outside. He looked familiar and Calvin stopped his horse. The man looked up.

'Howdy, marshal,' he said.

Calvin recognized him as the shotgun guard who had ridden the stagecoach which had brought him to Medicine Bend.

'Waitin' for a stage?' he joked.

The man spat on the ground in front of him. 'Stage is shut down,' he said. 'Ain't likely to run again while those outlaw varmints are still runnin' the show.'

'Times must be hard,' Calvin said.

'They sure are.'

Calvin had a sudden inspiration. 'How'd you like to do somethin' about it?' he said. The man's eyes were narrowed as he looked up at the marshal outlined against the sky.

'We're headin' for the hills right now, to smoke 'em out of their roost,' he added. 'We could use an extra gun.'

'You and Hurlock. Three of you,' Ransome remarked. 'I'd say you sure could.'

'Two,' Calvin replied. He pointed a thumb at Snell. 'This one's just along for the ride.'

Ransome burst into a laugh and began to splutter. He recovered sufficiently to spit a few times and then suddenly leaped to his feet.

'Are you serious?' he said.

'Deadly serious.'

The man thought for a few moments. 'Hell!' he exclaimed, 'Give me a chance to fetch my rifle and saddle up one of those hosses and I'll be right with you.' He turned and made for the corral. While they waited Calvin turned to Hurlock.

'You know him well?' he asked.

'Ransome? Sure thing. He's a good man to have around.'

'I remember him. He made his opinions of those varmints that attacked the stage pretty clear.'

It wasn't long till Ransome was back, carrying a rifle and leading a paint horse. He slipped the rifle into its scabbard and climbed into leather. He looked from Calvin to Hurlock and then at the troubled figure of Snell.

'What are we waitin' for, Marshal?' he asked. 'Let's go get 'em.'

Taber was enjoying himself, sometimes riding the mule and sometimes walking alongside it. The pace it set was slow but it seemed to suit him. It was in line with the changed tempo of his life. By mainly following the network of valleys, he had penetrated a considerable distance into the hills. He was still looking for a likely spot at which to begin to do some prospecting, but he wasn't too concerned to get down to serious digging. Even the warning he had been given by the group of prospectors he had come across didn't worry him unduly. He was a little more conscious of danger, but that was all.

The mule was going slowly; it was on an uphill slope leading to the crest of some rising ground. From time to time it stopped and Taber had to prompt it. He had grown fond of the animal and often spoke to it. He did so now, encouraging it to make a last effort to get to the top. When it finally arrived, Taber stopped to admire the view. As he did so, he suddenly saw a group of riders crossing an open stretch of ground in the distance. They didn't bother him because they were too far away, but something about them made him reach for his field-glasses to take a closer look. He put the glasses to his eyes and stared intently. After a few moments he put them down and mumbled something to himself before taking another look. He spent some time peering. The riders had their backs to him, but as he watched they turned and were sideways on. It was then that he definitely recognized two of the riders. They were the youngsters, Cora and Ricky, to whom he had been introduced by Miss Jowett at the Sycamore ranch. What were they doing here? He took a close look at the other four riders. Two of them were leading the youngsters' horses and he didn't at all like the way things appeared. He put the glasses down, but continued to watch, deep in thought, till they vanished almost suddenly from sight. He clapped the glasses back to his eyes but could not see what had become of them. A projecting wall of rock suggested they had gone round and behind it. He couldn't make any sense of the situation, but he felt instinctively that something was very wrong. He recalled the words of the prospectors. Could the youngsters have somehow fallen into the hands of renegades and outlaws? The more he thought about it, the more likely it seemed. What other answer could there be? Much more to the point, what was he to do about it?

Calvin and his little party made good progress. Snell certainly seemed to be familiar with the trails leading into the hills and Calvin couldn't help but think how long by comparison it would have taken to have attempted tracking Goad's gang – even if it could have been done. The posse had already tried that and had to give up the attempt pretty quickly. As they proceeded, he was more convinced than ever that he had made the right choice to ride in a small, tight party rather than with a posse. He guessed it had something to do with his time during the Civil War, when he had been part of a select cavalry unit often operating behind enemy lines. They had been able to inflict a lot of damage on the enemy then and he felt the same now. The main difference was that in those days Calvin had been familiar with the terrain, whereas here he was not. However, Hurlock had been up in the hills from time to time and knew enough to realise that the way Snell was leading them was not one of the more usual passages. He told Calvin as much and it seemed to both of them that this suggested that Snell was on the level rather than otherwise. In any case, he seemed to know his way. At one point, from the top of a pass, they were able to descry, a long way off, the stagecoach route. Snell still maintained his innocence. Calvin wasn't concerned about the extent of Snell's involvement. It was of no consequence. What mattered was dealing with the source of all the trouble – Goad – and eliminating him. Calvin felt a vague sense of irritation that Goad had ever been allowed out of jail to resume his murderous activities, but he himself was a representative of the law now and if that was the way it all panned out, well, that was the way it had to be.

The trail they were riding had narrowed and they rode single-file, with Snell leading the way and Hurlock bringing up the rear. After curving upwards it now took a down-turn before rising again to form a ridge. When they crested it and had more space, Snell stopped as the others came up.

'See over there,' he said, pointing towards a jutting shoulder of rock. They looked in the direction he indicated.

'What about it?' Calvin said.

'It's behind there that Gila has his stronghold in a

disused mining camp.'

'So we're almost there.'

'Yes, we're almost there.'

Calvin observed the outlaw closely. He was looking more worried than ever.

'I hope you aren't having any ideas about leaving us just yet,' he said. 'We might be close to Gila's camp, but we ain't there yet.' He drew out his field-glasses and swept the terrain.

'Sure is one hell of a view,' Ransome remarked.

'Who knows, there could be silver or gold in those ranges,' Hurlock mused.

They continued to sit their horses till Calvin put his field-glasses away and gave the order to carry on riding.

They started down the slope, moving carefully until they reached the bottom. Daylight was fading towards the west and shadows were creeping down from the higher reaches. Snell's knowledge was almost superfluous as the lay of the land dictated where they should ride and there was no other feasible trail. As the shadows deepened, Calvin began to consider the question of whether and where to make camp. Hearing the sound of running water and locating its source among some rocks and bushes a short distance from the trail, he drew to a halt.

'What do you reckon?' he asked Hurlock. 'If we're lookin' to set up camp, just here would be as good a place as any.'

'If that's what you're aimin' to do,' the oldster replied.

'You reckon we should push on?'

Hurlock shrugged. 'The closer we get, the more likely we are to be spotted. Especially if they've mounted guards. It might be better to carry on and get there when it's dark.'

Calvin called Snell over. 'How far is it now?' he asked.

'Not far. About three, maybe four hours' ride.'

Calvin thought for a moment, speculating on whether to follow Hurlock's suggestion and aim to arrive at the outlaw roost by night. It made a lot of sense. On the other hand, they had been riding for a long time and they were tired. If they carried on they could put the horses at some risk. It might be a better idea to stop and get some rest before starting on the final part of the trail early the next morning.

'Let's take a look,' he said. 'At least we can water the horses.'

One thing had been bothering him slightly. The outlaws were able to come and go quite readily and their tentacles reached as far as Medicine Bend. So far, the ride had been fairly straightforward but latterly it had got more difficult. If Snell was right, and they were getting close to Goad's hideout, he would expect to see some evidence of the fact. The outlaws seemed able to come and go pretty freely so their hideout should not be too remote. He still had some suspicions of Snell, but his doubts were soon laid to rest. As they veered off the track, Hurlock drew their attention to something by the side of the trail. They halted and Hurlock slid from the leather.

'Horse droppings,' he said, 'and not too old, by the look of it.'

Calvin nodded and, grinning, turned to Snell. 'Looks like we're on the right trail,' he said.

For a moment Snell looked offended. 'I told you I would show you the way,' he replied. 'Don't you trust me?'

Calvin didn't deign to reply. He couldn't help but notice how anxious Snell had become. It was one more sign that they were near their goal. Taken together with the evidence of the horse droppings, it was enough for him to make his mind up.

'We'll water the horses and take a break at the brook,' he said, 'and then carry on riding.'

Taber made what speed he could to cross the valley.

He realized that he was placing himself in an exposed position. If any other outlaws were to follow in the footsteps of the ones he had seen, they couldn't fail to spot him. He had to hope that the trail in and out of the valley on which he had seen them was not commonly used. As he moved, his eyes searched the terrain, looking out for riders. Gradually he got nearer to the place where he had seen the outlaws disappear. Taking out his field-glasses, he thought he detected an opening in the cliff face.

'Might not be anything,' he said to the mule. 'On the other hand, it could be a keyhole pass.'

If it was a gap, it was likely to be the entrance to a box canyon. There were probably many of them leading nowhere. On the other hand, if it did lead somewhere, it would be an ideal place to defend. He put himself in the position of the outlaws. If they were holed up somewhere, this would be the perfect back door. He raised the glasses and scanned the slopes. They were steep – too steep for a man to climb – so there would be no need for a guard. All the way across the valley he had been worried that the outlaws would have set sentries and as he got closer to the rock wall he had been half expecting a shot. He could see that there was clearly an opening leading into the cliff face at an acute angle. The entrance was narrow and dark and led upward quite steeply. He considered for a moment and then dismounted in order to lead the mule.

The pass was little more than a gash in the side of the mountain and the rock walls loomed high overhead, restricting the light. The trail took a turn and he was met with a blast of wind whistling down the canyon. It was an eerie place and it was with a sense of relief that Taber observed it was beginning to widen. He had been growing more and more concerned that it might not lead anywhere. Gradually the high rock walls began to recede and the shadows started to lift. The trail broadened further as it emerged into a high mountain valley and he carefully edged forward, making use of the cover provided by scattered rocks and boulders.

'Looks like we found where those varmints were taking Ricky and Cora,' he whispered to the mule.

Below him, under the shelter of a high peak, were some scattered buildings and behind them he could see a shaft which had been opened in the hillside. A thin feather of smoke curled upwards from one of the cabins and he could see some figures moving about. He spent a considerable time watching, looking out for any sign of the youngsters, but they didn't appear. It was a reasonable assumption that they were being held in one of the cabins, but which one? He needed to get close; the problem was how to do it without being detected. He looked about him at the hillsides. They were steep but he figured he could climb them. If he scrambled his way up, he should be able to work his way round to a point above the cabins without being seen. He could then climb down and get among the buildings, in one of which the youngsters were being held captive. Once he had made the decision, he set about making preparations for the climb.

It was dark inside the cabin in which they had been incarcerated and the youngsters were feeling frightened and miserable. They had been locked up for some time and they were hungry, too. The only thing the outlaws had given them since their arrival at the camp was a flask of water and a few strips of jerky. The enforced ride had been bad enough, but at least they had been out in the open and relatively free. Now they felt really trapped and at the mercy of their captors. Ricky tried to make a big effort to be brave and, putting his arm around his sister, he did his best to comfort her.

'What do they want?' she sobbed. 'What are they going to do to us?'

116

'Don't worry,' Ricky said, trying to convince himself as much as his sister. 'Once Father finds we're gone, he'll soon start looking. He'll find us.'

He took his arm from his sister and stood up in order to take another look at their surroundings. There wasn't much to see. The windows were encrusted with dirt and grime and it was very dark, particularly as the cabin lay in the shadow of the hillside. He tried the door once again but it was firmly barred. He tried pushing at it and then kicking it, but it didn't budge one inch. He knew it was hopeless, but he felt a need to do something. Maybe he could break one of the windows? He took off his shoe and began to hammer at it, but it showed no sign of breaking. Even if it did, the window was narrow; there was no way either of them could get through it. Frustrated, he bent down to put his shoe back on when he stopped short and listened closely. His sister was listening intently too so it was clear she had also heard something – a shuffling sound outside the door. She looked at him and he put his finger to his lips as an indication to keep quiet. At the same moment there came a rattle at the door and Cora sprang to her feet and ran to his side. She was shaking. The rattling stopped and then the door opened an inch or two and a figure slipped through, closing the door behind it. They had both had been expecting one of the outlaws but when they looked at the figure more closely, they could see that it was a woman.

'Don't be afraid,' she said, in a low voice. 'I won't hurt you.'

She came closer and touched Ricky on the arm. 'There's no time for explanations,' she whispered. 'If anyone finds I'm here . . .' She didn't continue but she didn't need to.

'Who are you?' Ricky breathed.

'My name is Lottie, but that doesn't matter. Just listen. In a few seconds I'm going, but I'll leave the door open. Wait a few minutes to give me time to get away; then slip out yourselves. Be careful there's no one around; then make your way to the entrance to the mine. A little way along there's a tunnel that runs up to the top of the hill. It's really an old ventilation shaft. It's quite steep but you're young. I think it's your best chance of getting away.'

Ricky and Cora exchanged glances, uncertain about whether to trust the woman. 'What do we do when we reach the top?' Ricky asked.

'You'll just have to take your chances.' She reached inside her dress. 'Here,' she said, taking out a small parcel, 'there's some food. It isn't much but it's the best I could do. There's also a stump of candle and some matches.'

Ricky was about to ask some further questions but she forestalled him by shaking her head and moving silently to the door. 'Remember to give me a couple of minutes,' she said and, before either of them could react, she was gone. Ricky moved to the door and peered out, but there was no sign of her. Night had fallen and he couldn't see very much. Quickly, he returned to his sister's side.

'What do we do?' she gasped.

'Just what she said,' he replied. 'What else can we do?'

They waited a few moments in silence, their nerves quivering. 'Come on,' he whispered. 'Stay close to me.'

She shrank back and he took her hand. 'We've got a chance this way,' he prompted. 'After all, things can't get worse than they are.'

He moved to the door and she followed, some-what reluctantly. He opened the door a little and stepped outside. After the gloom inside the shack, the night seemed almost bright. He looked carefully around but there was nobody about. A little way along he thought he could make out the entrance to the mine. Giving his sister's hand a squeeze, he began to move stealthily towards it. It took them only a matter of seconds to reach it, but when they were confronted by the gaping dark mouth of the tunnel, their courage failed them. Ricky looked about once more, wondering whether it might not be a better idea to ignore the woman's advice and carry on down the path. It certainly seemed a more attractive prospect than the black cavern in front of them and he might have been tempted to stay in the open, when he thought he heard the sound of footsteps. The next moment he saw a couple of shadowy figures moving towards them. There was no time for hesitation.

'Let's go,' he whispered. 'Somebody's coming.'

Holding tight his sister's hand, he took a step forward and entered the tunnel. There was sufficient light from outside for them to see their way at first, but soon the passage darkened and it was with difficulty that they picked their way. Then he remembered the candle. He struck one of the matches and held it to the wick but his hand was trembling and the flame went out before the candle caught alight. Making a conscious effort to steady his nerves, he tried again and this time the candle sputtered into life. It didn't give out very much illumination, but it was enough for them to see their way. Feeling a little more confident, they continued down the tunnel. They hadn't gone much further when they came to the entrance to another tunnel. Ricky held the candle out. The flame wavered and they both felt a draught of air.

'Do you think this is the shaft the woman meant?' Cora asked.

'I think it must be. Let's give it a try.'

The tunnel was narrower than the one they had been following and it got progressively steeper. They began to struggle and their breathing grew laboured. The air was freshening, however, and they could feel it on their faces. Suddenly, the candle went out, plunging them in darkness. For a few moments both of them felt panic begin to grip them but then Ricky saw a dim light ahead.

'Look,' he said, 'that must be the open air. The woman was right. Come on, keep going.'

Cora had seen it too and they pushed forward more hopefully, occasionally stumbling in the darkness. At one point the light vanished and their hearts sank, but it was only a bend in the tunnel and they soon saw it again. It was getting closer and closer, but still it seemed to take a long time to reach. They were panting for breath and their legs were shaking, but they were finally there and with a feeling of joy they emerged into the open air. Over their heads stars hung like jewels in the heavens and the breeze blew on their cheeks like a benediction. They stood doubled over, holding their sides and getting their breath back, before taking a good luck around them. They had come out on a ledge, not quite at the top of the hill. Down below, they could see the cabins. Once they had recovered from their exertions, Ricky pointed to a rough track which led the rest of the way up the hill.

'Better get moving,' he said. 'We want to get as far away as possible before they discover we're gone.'

At first the path was easy but it got gradually more difficult and it was not a simple matter to maintain their footing. At one point Cora slipped and would have gone sliding part of the way down the hill except that Ricky held her tight. A couple of times they approached what they thought was the top only to find that the path led further. When Ricky looked down, most of the outlaw camp remained in darkness, but he wondered how long it would take before their absence was noted. They were moving very slowly now; Cora especially was finding it a struggle.

'Nearly there,' Ricky gasped, to encourage her.

Cora was finding the last part of the trail very hard, but with Ricky's help she kept going. The path

seemed as if it would never end, but suddenly it lev-
elled off and a few more steps brought them of the
top of the hill. Both of them collapsing with the
strain, they lay there on their backs till they had
recovered and were feeling in control of themselves
again. Ricky looked at the cabins now even further
away below them. A light appeared moving across the
yard. It disappeared and then reappeared, together
with some other lights. Straining his eyes, Ricky
could distinguish shadowy forms of men moving
about and then they both heard a muted shout.

'I think they've discovered we're gone,' Ricky said.
Cora clung to his arm and in the starlight he could
see that she was frightened.

'Don't worry,' he said, 'They won't suspect we're
up here. All the same, maybe we'd better keep
moving.'

The night was luminous and they could see quite
clearly. They seemed to be on some sort of level
plateau with the dark shapes of hills outlined against
the sky; further off loomed higher mountain ranges.
Holding tight to each other, they began to walk.

It seemed to Calvin that they had been riding for
longer than three hours when Snell held up his arm
as a signal for them to stop.

'We're there,' he said.

Calvin peered ahead to the hill which reared its head against the skyline but could make nothing out.

'You'd better not be pullin' any stunts,' he said to Snell.

'I think I can see somethin',' Ransome said.

Calvin reached for his field-glasses and put them to his eyes. The mountainside came up close and as he lowered the glasses he made out the dim shadowy forms of buildings and then the entrance to a tunnel. Scanning the bottom of the hill, he saw horses in a corral a little further along. He put the glasses down and passed them to Hurlock to take a look.

'You got us here,' Calvin said to Snell. 'Your part of the bargain is done. You don't have to stay. We've got no objections if you turn right round and go.'

Snell's head hung and even in the dark, Calvin couldn't help but notice the unhappy expression on the outlaw's face.

'What are you all gonna do now?' Snell asked.

'Deal with Goad.'

Snell laughed mirthlessly. 'How are you gonna do that?' he said. 'There are three of you against Gila and his entire gang.'

'You don't need to concern yourself about it,' Calvin replied. 'That's our problem, not yours.'

Snell gave Calvin a look on which anguish, disbelief and misery vied for pre-eminence. He threw a look towards Goad's hideout as if searching for some kind of sign and it seemed that it was given. Suddenly, lights began to appear, moving about like fireflies.

'What can you see?' Calvin snapped, addressing Hurlock.

'Somethin's goin' on. There are men runnin' about. Here, take a look yourself.'

He handed the glasses to Calvin who peered through them intently. A number of people had appeared on the scene, carrying torches. As he watched, some of them began to move towards the corral and presently he saw riders start to spread out. The sound of hoof beats carried on the still night air. Instantly, he saw an opportunity.

'I don't know what's happened,' he said, 'but something's disturbed them. We could get right up there without being detected. If they see us, they might even think we're part of the gang.'

'Maybe it's us they've seen,' Snell mumbled.

Calvin glanced at him. Could Snell have given them some kind of signal? No sooner had the thought crossed his mind than he rejected it. Hurlock and Ransome looked at one another dubiously and then Ransome burst into a laugh.

'Hell,' he said, 'we've come this far so we might as well go the rest of the way.'

'What do we do if we get as far as their hideout?' Hurlock asked.

'Pray,' Ransome said.

Calvin tried to think of a reasoned reply but realized he didn't have one to give. His face creased in a wry grin.

'Come on,' he said. 'Let's ride.'

Almost as one, they spurred their horses, moving quickly into a gallop. As they charged forward, Calvin realized he had clean forgotten Snell. He looked back over his shoulder but he couldn't see whether the outlaw remained or whether he had gone. There was no time to waste thinking about him. Snell could take his chances the same as everyone else. As he rode he looked about, trying to take stock of the situation. Here and there he could see flickering flames that indicated where a few of the riders were carrying torches, but they soon faded and he could see nothing of the outlaws. He couldn't work out what could have happened to stir them into action, but clearly something had occurred. A more important question was how many of them remained behind, and would Goad be among them? They were riding hard and covering the distance to the outlaw stronghold pretty quickly. He could see much better now the layout of the camp and its relation to the surrounding terrain. He doubted whether anyone would detect them in the dark and confusion so he kept on riding till he was quite close to the camp when he gave the signal for them to halt. He slid from the saddle and the others did likewise.

'I figure that's far enough,' he whispered. 'We'll sneak up on 'em the rest of the way. Stay together.'

Taking their rifles from their scabbards, they crept forward, keeping low and taking advantage of any scrap of vegetation they could. It was to their advantage that the movement of people had abated. Once only a couple of figures appeared from one of the huts and made their way in the direction of the corral, but otherwise the area was deserted. Calvin looked closely at the various structures comprising the camp, trying to decide which one in particular Goad might be likely to use as his own. One of them was decidedly bigger than the others and another stood at a little distance from the rest of the camp. He wasn't sure which of them to aim for. They were getting close to their target and they remained undetected even though the night was clear, but between them and the cabins there was an open stretch of ground that offered little in the way of cover. They drew to a halt to consider the situation and Calvin had just about made up his mind to take the risk of crossing it when they heard the sound of voices and out of the darkness a group of men appeared. There was no time to move away; all they could do was to drop to the ground and lie flat. Only the short stretch of open ground separated them and they were able to hear quite clearly what the men were saying to each other.

'Where the hell can they be?'

'I don't know, but they can't have got far.'

'Where's Gila? Is he still with the girl?'

'I've no idea, but I figure we'd better get searchin' again.'

Calvin raised his head. A couple of the men were staring out across the open ground straight in their direction, and he anticipated the worst. It seemed that they must be detected, but after a few more moments the men moved on. Calvin glanced towards the others. Ransome seemed as if he was beginning to move but Calvin indicated for him to remain still. From somewhere a dog began to snarl and he heard the clank of a chain as the animal pulled on it. He felt a frisson of concern. What if a Gila lizard wasn't the only creature that Goad kept? He heard the faint mumbling of a voice and the snarling ceased. They continued to lie flat till Calvin figured they were as safe from being spotted as they were likely to be and finally gave the signal for them to move on. He had selected the small cabin as the place to aim for. Followed closely by the others, he began to creep forward and soon reached it.

He pulled at the door but it was locked. He took a moment to think and then swung his leg and kicked it. In a matter of seconds the wood splintered and gave way and he rushed inside. Hurlock and Ransome came up behind him and they stood for a moment, trying to make out their surroundings, till Ransome moved towards the back of the cabin.

'We'd better decide quickly what we do next,' Hurlock said. 'It wouldn't do to get trapped in here.'

'We're fine for the moment,' Calvin replied.

There was a sudden exclamation from Ransome and then he gave a low chuckle. 'Gentlemen,' he said, 'I think we may have struck lucky.'

'What do you mean?' Calvin replied.

'Come over here and take a look.'

Puzzled, they crossed to where he stood beside a pile of crates. One of them was open and Calvin bent down to take a look inside. At the bottom of the crate were some objects that looked like round cakes and a pile of black powder.

'What is it?' he asked.

'Gunpowder. There's no way of knowin' how long it's been there or what sort of condition it's in. There are fuses too, and a funnel for pourin'.'

Calvin straightened up. 'I guess it must have been left over from when this place was a workin' mine.'

'If we needed any further proof about who carried out that bank job, I think we've got it now,' Hurlock commented.

'Well, wherever it came from, I think it's maybe time those outlaw varmints got a taste of their own medicine,' Ransome replied.

Calvin was about to respond when suddenly he thought he heard a sound. He glanced at the others. They had heard it too. They all listened intently and then it came again, a soft murmur like someone breathing. It seemed to be coming from behind some of the boxes in the far corner. Calvin drew his gun and stepped across. Behind the boxes he could see a dark shape, cowering very low.

'Get on your feet!' he snapped.

The crouching figure shuffled and then slowly stood upright. To his surprise and consternation, it was of a woman.

'Who are you?' Calvin said.

'More to the point, what's she doin' here?' Hurlock added.

The woman's gaze darted from one to another. 'You are not with Gila,' she managed to say. The remark was more of a statement than a question.

'No, we ain't. In fact, just the opposite,' Calvin replied. Looking closely at the woman, he could see that her face was bruised and bloodied.

'Did Goad do that to you?' he asked. As if she had only just noticed her injuries, she put her hand to her face.

'It's OK,' Calvin continued, trying to reassure her. 'You have nothing to fear from us.'

'The children,' she said. 'Have you come for the children?'

'Children?' Calvin queried.

'Not children maybe. Young people. Gila's men are out looking for them now.'

Calvin looked towards the others and then back at the girl. She took a tottering step forward and as he held out his arms, she fell into them.

'I think perhaps you'd better tell us just who you are and what's goin' on here,' he said gently.

CHAPTER SIX

Ricky and Cora hadn't gone very far when they stopped in their tracks. From somewhere out in the night, they both thought they had heard something.

'What was that?' Cora asked.

Ricky suspected it was the sound of horses but he didn't want to scare his sister by saying so. 'I don't know,' he replied. 'It's probably just some night bird.' He was trying to reassure her, but he didn't feel very reassured himself. If there was a way up for riders from the valley below, they could be in deep trouble.

'Come on,' he said, 'we'd better keep going.'

They stumbled on. Ricky's intention was simply to put as much space between them and the outlaw roost as possible. He had seen the horsemen set out from the disused mine, but it hadn't occurred to him previously that they might appear on top of the plateau. How long would it take them? As time passed he began to grow more hopeful, but suddenly his ears picked up the sound again and this time there was no fooling Cora.

'They're coming,' she said, grabbing his arm in fear. 'What are we going to do now?'

He looked about frantically for a place to hide but there was little in the way of cover. All they could hope to do was to stay low and hope the outlaws missed them in the dark. Quickly but gently, he pulled Cora down to the ground as he caught a first sight of a pair of riders coming towards them. Cora was shaking and beginning to sob.

'Try and be quiet,' he said. 'We don't want them to hear us.'

He was trying to be brave and for a few moments he thought the riders had veered away, but he was soon disillusioned as they swung back and came rapidly on. The horses' hoofs drummed louder and louder and Rick thought they were about to be trampled when they came to a sudden halt. There was a thud as the riders dismounted and then rough hands seized them and dragged them to their feet.

'You little. . . !' a voice snarled without finishing

the sentence. Instead, it was accompanied by a savage blow to the side of Ricky's head, which sent him crashing back to earth. His sister screamed but she was quickly silenced when the other outlaw clapped his hand across her mouth. She found it hard to breathe and instinctively bit him. With a gasp he spun her round and hit her hard across the cheek.

'I think they need to be taught a lesson,' he said.

He drew his hand back as she cowered away and Ricky struggled to his feet to try and protect her. Before the hand could fall, a voice suddenly rang out from the darkness.

'Leave them alone! Try anything and you're dead.'

The outlaws glanced at one other in surprise and then simultaneously they reached for their guns, turning and flinging themselves sideways as they did so. They shot into the dark from which stabs of flame lit up the night as someone opened fire in reply. Ricky grabbed his sister and dragged her to the ground. One of the outlaws was lying inert a few feet away and the other was down on one knee, firing rapidly but blindly. Another shot rang out and he toppled over and lay still. After the sudden uproar, the silence was almost as deafening. Ricky, lying on top of his sister to protect her, stared into the gloom. He didn't know what to expect, but he feared the worst. Out of the darkness the shadowy figure of a man emerged, a smoking gun in his hand. He advanced to where the two outlaws lay and bent over them. Then he stood up and put his gun back into its holster.

'Is that you – Ricky . . . Cora?' the man said. Ricky tried to speak but his throat was too dry and only a kind of cackle emerged.

'Don't be afraid. I'm not one of the outlaws. I'm here to rescue you.' The man came forward and it seemed to Ricky that there was something familiar about him.

'My name is Taber. I'm a friend of your aunt. You might remember meeting me.'

Something clicked in Ricky's mind and he recognized the stranger. His voice came back, thick and hoarse.

'Mr Taber,' he repeated. 'Mr Taber.' He bent his head close to his sister. 'It's Mr Taber,' he said. 'Remember him? It's Mr Taber. We're safe now.'

The night was quiet, but Calvin knew it was only a matter of time till the outlaws searching for Ricky and Cora returned. If he was to take advantage of their absence, he and his companions needed to act quickly. Fortunately, the woman had quietened down

135

and they had managed to clean up her wounds. Calvin was in a quandary about what their next move should be. After listening to her story, he was particularly concerned about the well-being of the youngsters.

'Right now we've got an edge,' he said to Hurlock, 'because the outlaws don't know we're here. But pretty soon those riders are gonna be back and then our position's gonna be real precarious.'

Hurlock glanced at the crates of gunpowder. 'Seems a pity not to make use of it,' he said.

'Do you know anythin' about explosives?' Calvin replied.

The oldster shook his head. 'Nope, but I'd be willin' to learn.'

'Yeah, and blow us all up in the process!'

Just then Ransome stepped forward. 'I know how to use it,' he said. 'It's been a while, but I once did some minin' and we used it then.'

Calvin didn't reply. His brain was working rapidly and he was already hatching out a plan. 'Listen,' he said, 'this is how I see things. Those outlaw varmints are down on their numbers temporarily and we've got the element of surprise on our side. I figure we should have just enough time to rig up a few explosions – enough to put this place out of action. Once we've done that, we have no option but to go after the youngsters.'

'I figure I could set the fuses to blow once we reach the top of the hill, if that's what we're aimin' to do,' Ransome said.

'You heard what Lottie said. That's where the youngsters were headed.' He glanced at the woman. 'Do you understand what we're sayin'?' he asked.

'Yes,' she replied, 'and you don't need to worry about me, if that's what you're drivin' at. In fact, I can help. I know this place and might be able to show you the best spots to lay the fuses. I can guide you to the top of the hill.'

Calvin had been worried that she might be suffering some kind of reaction after her experiences, but she seemed quite ready and willing to take part.

'OK,' he replied. He turned back to Ransome. 'Go ahead. Show us what we have to do.'

At that very moment Gila was fuming with a sense of frustration. The youngsters had escaped and he thought he knew who was responsible. Lottie had herself gone missing. She was hiding somewhere and once he found her, he meant to deal with her in a way she would never forget if she even survived. It wouldn't just be a beating this time. No, it would be something to really teach her a lesson. He expected his men to return very soon with the youngsters in tow. He would deal with them, too, but he would be careful not to cause any lasting damage. After all, they were still his bargaining counters for gaining control of the Sycamore ranch. Really, he was being too considerate. It might have been much simpler just to launch an assault on the place. Jowett and his miserable cow-hands wouldn't have been able to offer much in the way of resistance.

On top of these immediate considerations, he still had the question of how he was to deal with Calvin. It would have to involve the maximum of pain and suffering. That was the least Calvin owed him for all the time he had spent in the penitentiary. With so much on his mind, he was feeling restless. He stood beside the cage in which the Gila monster was housed, talking to it in barely repressed tones of anger, when he suddenly turned on his heels and made for the door. Outside the night was quiet after the shooting which had gone on previously. A couple of men were passing by outside, looking for the escapees, and he called them over.

'What's happenin'?' he said. 'Haven't those two been found yet?'

'Nothin' so far,' one of the men replied, 'but we'll get 'em.'

'You'd better. They must be around somewhere.'

'It won't take much longer,' the man replied nervously. It was impossible to tell how Gila might react. 'Once the others get back, we'll soon flush 'em out.'

He feared he might have said the wrong thing, but Gila didn't respond. Instead, his eyes searched the darkness. He was reluctant to mention the girl and the part he was convinced she had played in freeing the prisoners in case it reflected on himself. For a moment he thought he saw a flicker of movement, but he decided it was nothing more than a fleeting impression.

'What are you two waitin' around for?' Gila snapped. He paused, his jaw working, then he turned and, without further comment, went back inside. The men looked at each other and decided the sensible thing would be to move away. They had a vague sense that, somehow, they'd just had a lucky escape. They didn't suspect it was because Goad was stressed and feeling a need for the companionship of the Gila lizard.

In and out of the shadows, keeping to the darker areas and ever alert to the slightest sign of danger,

Ransome and his helpers laid the gunpowder. It was easier than Calvin would have expected, and he figured it wasn't just down to the fact that they had caught the outlaws at an awkward time. The way he saw it, Goad was so confident and self-assured that he didn't even anticipate someone might find his outlaw roost. That was why he hadn't bothered to set out any guards on the approaches to it. That overweening hubris was all in their favour. It was still a dangerous enterprise and he wasn't the only one who could feel his nerves jingle. Fortunately, they had Lottie to guide them and it made a lot of difference. She knew her way about the camp. She knew which areas to avoid and she knew the practices and habits of the outlaws so that there was less danger of running into any of them who had remained behind.

They worked quickly, following Ransome's instructions, choosing crevices and cracks in the rock wall where an explosion might be expected to cause the greatest damage. The black powder was poured in using the small funnel they had found in the cabin, and then the fuse placed in it. Ransome corkscrewed the fuse into the powder for an inch or so.

'I don't know the burn rate of the fuse,' he whispered. 'When I light it, just make sure you ain't anywhere near.'

'I don't intend to be,' Hurlock replied.

Ransome grinned and carried on with his task, backfilling the hole with clay and tamping it down. While they worked, the woman stood guard. At one point they heard footsteps approaching and stood back in the shelter of the cliff wall while one of the outlaws walked past within a few yards of them. After what seemed an eternity they had finished placing the gunpowder.

'We're about ready,' Ransome stated. 'Like I said, it's hard to know how long the fuses will burn, but I've set them to give us five minutes or so leeway. I've also tried to stagger them.'

'Right,' Calvin said. He glanced at the others. 'OK. Let's do it.'

Ransome lit the first fuse and then they quickly made their way to the next one. It only took a matter of seconds and when they had lit them all they quickly made their way to the tunnel entrance. Hurlock and the woman had already ducked inside when there was a sudden shout and the next moment the night was lit up by a stab of flame and the reverberation of gunfire echoed around the camp.

'You carry on!' Calvin screamed. 'I'll try an' hold 'em up.'

Ransome paused, but Calvin ushered him away. Reluctantly, Ransome vanished down the tunnel. Calvin placed himself in the entrance, taking cover behind the rock wall. There was a lot of shouting going on and almost immediately a barrage of gunfire opened up. Bullets sang and whined as they ricocheted off the rock and he felt blood running down his face where he had been hit by a shard. Taking advantage of a momentary cessation, he leaned forward and began blasting away with his rifle, quickly pulling back again as a fresh round of fire opened up in reply. He looked back but couldn't see any sign of the others.

Bullets were raining in now from all sides and he was thankful that it was night otherwise, despite the protection of the projecting rock-wall, he would surely have been hit. He needed to hold the outlaws back for just a little while longer to give his companions a decent head start, but his position was rapidly becoming untenable. His rifle was empty and he flung it down. Drawing one of his six-guns, he squeezed the trigger, aiming for the flashes as the outlaws fired. There was another crescendo of gunfire and he saw the shapes of men running forward. They were closer than he had allowed for and he knew he had left it too late to get away. He was about to be overwhelmed. Still, he meant to sell his life dearly.

It was just as he had resigned himself to his inevitable fate that the scene in front of him exploded in fire and flames with a shock that shook the ground. The noise was deafening and he reeled back in confusion. It took him a few moments to realize what had happened. In the rack and furore of battle he had forgotten all about the gunpowder. Another explosion sent him staggering and then he began to run down the tunnel. He felt disoriented. Despite this, he possessed just enough of his senses to remember to look for the air shaft, but where was it? He couldn't find it! He was stumbling in the dark and was suddenly brought up short when he collided into the wall of the tunnel. He fell over, stunned with the force of the impact, and remained still for some time, waiting for his strength to return. He knew he wasn't badly hurt. Apart from the cut to his face, his shoulder ached; as he lay he flexed his gun hand and it quickly responded. After the loud impact of the explosion, things seemed preternaturally quiet and he began to think.

The explosions had been big. There was no way of knowing, but with any luck the outlaw roost should have been put out of action. Goad's men had taken the full force of the blast, but what about Goad himself? Had he been killed or could he have survived? Calvin had come to Medicine Bend to rid it of outlaws, and he reckoned he had done that. It was only after his arrival that he had found out about Goad. But when he had ridden out of town with Hurlock and Ransome, their target was Goad: especially so for Calvin, after what had happened to Dolores. And he had no proof that Goad had been eliminated. Until he had that proof, the job was incomplete. He needed to know what had happened to Goad. As he weighed the matter up, he suddenly remembered what Snell had told him about Goad's habit of retiring to his special hideout, the cave where he liked to be alone. Maybe Goad had been blown sky-high, but if he had survived the blasts where would he retreat to? What place more likely than the cave? It was still a long shot. He might have left the scene altogether. He might not even have been there in the first place. But it was worth taking a look.

Gingerly, he struggled back to his feet. He took a moment to consider which way he should go and then began to move slowly down the tunnel, taking great care and inching his way along. An acrid smell of smoke reached his nostrils and he pulled up his bandana to protect himself from the gathering dust which he sensed was filling the tunnel. He saw a shimmering light which flickered on the walls and heard a faint crackling sound, and he quickly realized this was the noise of fire. Gasping for breath, he arrived back at the mouth of the tunnel and stumbled into the open.

It was a lurid scene which met his eyes. Buildings were burning and the night sky was filled with sparks. Smoke billowed. Scattered about were the charred and mangled remains of outlaws. He looked about for signs of activity, but nobody was to be seen. He moved away from the tunnel entrance and began walking, looking out for the mouth of a cave in which he might find Goad. He could not remember having seen one while they were laying the gunpowder, so he set his course in the opposite direction to the hut which had been their immediate refuge. The flames roared and hissed behind him like the cackling of the demons of the place; once he heard a distant voice, but the further he moved away from the main buildings, the more confident he became that he would remain undetected. His keen eyes sought for the cave that Snell had mentioned. It could be anywhere. Maybe it was higher up the cliff face and there was a way into it which only Goad knew. All he could do was to keep his eyes open. Then, just as he was thinking he must have gone too far, he saw it; a dark, ugly slit in the face of the cliff.

As he got closer he thought he could hear a thin droning noise and presently he detected a faint gleam of light. He stopped to take a good look around. The night was lit up by the burning buildings behind him and illuminated by the glimmering light of stars. Away off in the distance he thought for a moment that he detected the dim shadowy outlines of a couple of riders, but though he stared hard, they didn't materialize. If they were horsemen, he concluded, they were probably a remnant of the outlaws who had ridden out earlier. He waited a while longer, concealed by the shadow of the cliff face, listening to the faint droning. He wasn't sure what it could be; maybe it was just an effect of the night breeze. With a last glance behind him, he crept forward again.

The droning sound grew louder and then he realized it was a voice, but it was hard to make anything out clearly. When he was almost up to the mouth of the cave he stopped to listen closer. It was definitely a voice, speaking in little above a whisper in a strange, piping sibilant. He leaned forward, straining his ears, trying to pick out individual words. Who was in there? Was it Goad? If so, to whom was he talking? His every nerve was strained as he tried to make out

any change of tone which might indicate that a conversation was taking place. He began to pick out what
sounded like odd words and phrases:

You and me . . . stick together . . . nobody else.

He thought back to his conversation with Snell.
Suddenly he realized that it must be Goad inside the
cave; he was indeed having a conversation of sorts,
but not with any fellow human. He was talking to the
Gila lizard.

My beauty . . . feed. . . . Then he heard his own
name mentioned. *Calvin . . . must be . . . slice.*

Calvin didn't wait to hear any more. Drawing his
six-gun, he crept stealthily into the mouth of the
cave.

Immediately he was inside, his nostrils were
assailed by a fetid smell which made his gorge rise.
He pulled up his bandana and slipped forward,
keeping close to the wall on which a flickering candle
cast eerie shadows. Then, at the back of the cave, he
saw the figure of a man, sitting on its heels and
rocking gently to and fro. He was cradling something
in his hand; it took a moment for Calvin to register
that it was the lizard. He watched in fascination as the
man lifted something with his other hand and put it
in the lizard's mouth. In the guttering light of the
candle he saw the lizard's head jerk and then a slight

but distinctive undulation of its body as it swallowed whatever the man had given it. A few moments later its tongue flicked out and the man reached into his pocket. Calvin had seen enough.

'Goad!' he rasped. 'The game's up!'

The response was unexpected. No sooner were the words out of his mouth than the candle was extinguished and darkness filled the cavern. There was a sound of footsteps and something brushed past him, knocking him to one side. By the time he had recovered his balance, the steps had died away. For a few more moments his eyes remained blinded and then a gleam of light filtering from the night outside showed him the way to the cave entrance. He looked up and down but could see no-one. To his right the buildings were still burning, but the flames had dwindled. He decided to go in the opposite direction, but hadn't got far when he heard the clatter of hoofs and, looking up, saw a rider silhouetted against the night sky. The vision lasted for a moment and then the hoof-beats dwindled away. He began to run and soon saw the dark outline of the corral. A couple of horses remained, both of them saddled. Choosing the nearest one, he vaulted into leather, dug in his spurs and set off in the same direction he had seen Goad depart.

He rode hard, taking no heed of the dangers presented by the darkness. He was keen to make up the lost ground, and was soon rewarded by the sight of a rider going hell-for-leather ahead of him. He had no way of being completely certain that he had his man, but he was pretty sure it was Goad. Although Goad was going fast, he was gradually making ground on him. He looked around in order to get a sense of his bearings. They were heading across the floor of a valley towards what looked like a solid wall of rock. Glancing over his shoulder, he could see the outlaw camp still burning. He was brought up sharp when his horse almost stumbled, and to try and avoid further trouble he slowed up a little. Goad seemed to have gained some ground. It was hard to tell in the dark, but as the chase continued he kept his target steadily in his sights as they hurtled on, pace for pace. The sound of his horse's hoofs beat a regular tattoo and he was pretty sure that Goad must have heard him. Then, quite suddenly, he lost sight of his quarry.

Calculating that he had probably gone down into a dip, he carried on riding and was rewarded after a short time by a further view of the fleeing horseman before he vanished again. This time he did not reappear and it was evident that he must have veered off and found cover somewhere. Looming up ahead of him was a ridge of rock formations and boulders backed by a stand of trees and thickets into which Goad must have ridden.

Quickly, he drew the horse to a stop. The animal was breathing heavily and its nostrils were full of foam. It would have been cruel to attempt to ride it much further. But if his horse was in an exhausted state, so must Goad's be also. He strained his ears to listen for the sound of hoof-beats, and as he did so the roar of a rifle rang out and something slammed into his saddle-horn, sending up splinters of leather. The horse reared and as it did so he slid from the saddle, landing hard and narrowly avoiding its flailing hoofs. He knew he had been stupid, presenting himself as a target. Goad had not gone into the trees. He had taken up a position among the rocks from which he could bushwhack his pursuer. It was sheer luck, combined with the fact that he had stopped short, that had saved him.

As further shots rang out, Calvin rolled into the shelter of the undergrowth and drew his six-gun. From the flashes accompanying the gun shots, he had a general idea of where Goad was hiding. It wasn't very helpful. Goad still had the advantage. He was well concealed and could move about among the rocks. From his vantage point, he had a pretty good overview of the surrounding terrain. Calvin was to some extent pinned down. Goad had a rifle and he only had his six-gun. To have any chance, he needed to get closer, but the vegetation was thin and any movement would be likely to be detected. He had only a vague idea of what time it was, but the dawn couldn't be too far off. Night-time was his friend. If he was to get close to Goad, he needed to do it while it was dark.

He began to crawl away but hadn't gone far when Goad's rifle boomed again and a bullet went whistling over his head. He lay flat, and was about to try and move on when the night was pierced by a high-pitched voice which rang eerily across the valley.

'I know who you are, Calvin. I know your game.'

Calvin raised his head from the ground, trying to catch a glimpse of Goad, but could see nothing.

'I don't know what you're doin' here, Calvin, but you ain't gonna get away. You're a fool to think you could match yourself against me.'

Calvin thought for a moment. It probably wasn't wise to give his position away any further by replying, but he couldn't resist the challenge.

'Take a look at your hideout, Goad. There ain't much left of it.'

'You dirty low-down rattlesnake. I'll kill you and

feed you piece by piece to my lizard.'

'I heard about your lizard. It's a beast, Goad, a dumb beast. It don't like you, it don't care for you. It just don't give a damn.'

There was a shattering explosion as Goad loosed off a couple of shots by way of reply, but Calvin sensed they were not as close as the previous salvo.

'Give yourself up, Goad. That way I might just pardon the lizard.'

'You keep your dirty hands off. I'm tellin' you.'

'You're tellin' me what?'

'You and your kind; you're all the same. You deserve to die. I'm gonna cut you into thin strips of meat and feed them to the lizards and the buzzards and the coyotes. You're gonna die real slow. I'm gonna slice you up, you and that woman, I'm gonna slice you and dice you and make you bleed.'

Calvin didn't reply. Instead, as Goad continued to rant, he continued edging his way in the direction of the rocks, half-expecting Goad to see him and open fire again, but the shots didn't come. He didn't have too much further to go. Goad's voice continued to ring out, but suddenly it changed to a high-pitched moaning. It was a frightening sound and Calvin involuntarily shrank back, pressing himself hard against the ground. The moaning grew louder until it became a long drawn out scream.

'You made him do it, Calvin!' Goad shrieked. 'You turned him against me.'

There was a moment's silence and then the night was riven by a series of explosions as Goad opened fire randomly. He was blazing away yet even above the noise the sounds of his screams could be heard. Sensing that something had happened to make Goad finally flip, Calvin drew his gun, got to his feet and, bent double, ran for the shelter of the rocks. He had almost reached them when the figure of Goad appeared, staggering forwards and blazing away with the rifle. Calvin felt a sharp jolt of pain and his gun fell from his hand. At the same time Goad's rifle seemed to jam and he threw it away from him as he turned to face Calvin.

'You killed him, Calvin. It was you, not me. You made him turn against me. I had to do it, but it's you to blame.'

Calvin didn't know what Goad was raving on about, and then realized that he was referring to the Gila lizard. He moved towards the outlaw and saw that blood was running down his chin from a wound to his upper lip.

'He wouldn't have bitten me. It was you made him do it.'

Suddenly Goad threw himself forward and before Calvin could draw his gun the crazed outlaw chief was on top of him. The force of the impact threw them both over, but Goad was quicker on his feet. As Calvin tried to stand, Goad's boot crashed into his chin and he went down again. His head hit the ground hard and he was momentarily stunned. He saw a flash of light and realized Goad had drawn a knife. He flung up an arm to protect himself as Goad landed on top of him. The man's face was twisted in a rage of fury and hatred and his eyes were wide. He lifted the knife again, but Calvin managed to seize hold of his wrist. For a few moments he succeeded in holding Goad's knife hand aloft, but the man was possessed and slowly but inexorably the knife began to descend till it was only inches from his throat.

'You're gonna die! I'm gonna slice you!' Goad screamed.

His eyes were gleaming and foam stood at the corners of his mouth. Blood dripped from the bite to his lip. In desperation Calvin reached out with his wounded hand and felt something cold and solid. It was a stone and with a last frantic effort he lifted it and brought it crashing down on Goad's head. Goad yelled but his grip on the knife relaxed and Calvin was able to push him back. They were both on their feet at the same time. Goad slashed with the knife but Calvin danced aside and, catching Goad slightly off balance, delivered a hard blow to the outlaw's stomach. Goad gasped and Calvin followed it up with a swingeing blow to the side of Goad's head which sent him reeling back. Calvin dived forward, planting his head hard in the outlaw's midriff, and they fell to the ground again. This time, however, it was Calvin who had the advantage as he began to rain blow upon blow to Goad's face. Suddenly he felt a sharp pain and realised Goad had stabbed him in the side. Gasping with the shock of it, he leaped up and swung his boot, attempting to kick the knife from the outlaw's hand. He made contact but lost his balance and toppled backwards. When he had steadied himself he saw Goad coming at him still holding the knife. Goad lunged forward and as Calvin dropped to one knee, Goad went head over heels over the top of him. Calvin immediately swung round to face him but Goad lay still. Calvin waited for a moment, but there was no sign of movement; only a thin stream of blood appeared from underneath the outlaw. Calvin sprang to his side and turned him over. Goad's eyes stared up unseeing into the fading night and his face was twisted in a permanent grimace of hatred and pain. He had landed on his own knife.

When he was sure that Goad was dead, Calvin got to his feet and, staggering to the nearest boulder, sat down on it. He was exhausted and he was hurt, but he knew enough to realize that the knife wound was not serious. He examined his hand. A red streak showed where a bullet had creased the palm. Then he pulled aside his shirt to look at the wound in his side. The knife had bitten quite deep, but his thick jacket had saved him from something worse. When he had recovered a little, he staunched the bleeding with his bandana and then got to his feet. The first glimmerings of dawn were in the sky as he made his way back to his horse. He clambered aboard and then sat for a few minutes trying to decide what to do next. His first instinct was to return to the devastated outlaw camp but then he had a change of plan. The sides of the valley in places were not steep and it should be perfectly possible to ride the horse up to the top of the plateau. Once up there, he would set about finding the others.

The lights were blazing at the Sycamore ranch house. Jowett had thrown a party to celebrate the return of Ricky and Cora. It was late and the youngsters had finally gone to bed, leaving the invited guests to talk.

'I was worried about that gunpowder,' Ransome

said. 'There was no way of knowin' what condition it was in. It might not even have gone off.'

'I'd say it worked well enough,' Calvin commented. He eased himself in his chair to relieve the pressure on the bandage which was wrapped around his side.

'Those owlhoots are never goin' to be usin' that place again,' Hurlock remarked. 'If there's any of 'em left, that is.'

'If there are any, they won't be causin' any more trouble round these parts,' Ransome said. 'Not without Goad.' He looked at the marshal. 'You were plumb lucky to come out of that business alive,' he added. 'You shouldn't have gone after him alone.'

'There was no time to beat about the bush,' Calvin replied. 'It was just a hunch that Goad might be still around in that cave. I needed to act quickly.'

Hurlock laughed. 'Hell,' he said, 'we must have been crazy ridin' into that nest of snakes.'

'You mean lizards,' Ransome said.

'Lizards . . . snakes . . . whatever you like to call the varmints. They must still be wonderin' just what hit 'em.'

'Most of 'em were probably like Snell,' Calvin said, 'lookin' to find a way out.' His words made the others pause and think for a moment.

'Snell,' Hurlock remarked, 'I'd forgotten all about him. Well, I guess he's probably gone way to hell by now. Good luck to him.'

Taber smiled. 'I guess in a way you could say he turned out to be our insurance policy.'

The others turned to him with uncomprehending looks on their faces, but Taber was spared the necessity of explaining his remark when Miss Jowett appeared in the doorway.

'Would you gentlemen like some coffee?' she asked.

'Sure thing,' Hurlock replied. He glanced at the empty bottle of whiskey which stood on a table. 'And I'd say we could do with lots of it.'

'Coming right up,' she replied.

When she had gone Calvin turned to Ransome. 'I hear the stagecoach is startin' up again. You'll have your old job back.'

'Yup. But somehow I don't think I'm gonna be kept too busy now Goad and his gang are gone.'

'What about you?' Calvin continued, addressing Taber. 'Are you headin' back for those hills?'

Taber thought for a moment. 'I don't know,' he replied. 'I figure maybe I ain't cut out for prospectin' after all.'

'What'll you do? Go back to sellin' insurance?'

Taber shook his head. 'I ain't so sure about that either,' he said. 'No, maybe I'll just stick around and try my hand at somethin' else.'

'You could try ranchin',' Jowett said. 'There's always room for a good man right here at the Sycamore.'

Taber turned his head as Miss Jowett returned with the coffee on a tray. 'You know,' he said, 'I might just take you up on that.'

Miss Jowett put the tray down and began to pour the thick black liquid. When she had done so, she sat down beside her nephew.

'Lottie is sleeping,' she said. 'She seems to be making a good recovery.'

'It was real nice of you to offer her a place to stay till she finds her feet again,' Calvin remarked to Jowett.

'She can stay as long as she likes,' the rancher replied.

'I figure there might be a place for her at the Eating House,' Calvin added. 'I've had a word with Dolores and she might be glad of a little help.'

'At least Ricky and Cora seem to be none the worse for their experiences,' Miss Jowett said.

Her nephew was thoughtful for a moment. 'They're young and resilient. In no time at all they'll regard the whole thing as a bit of an adventure,' he finally replied.

'Besides,' Taber said, addressing Miss Jowett, 'they've got you to keep an eye on them.'

'I don't think they really need me. They're growing up into fine young people.'

'We all need you,' Jowett remarked, 'Ricky and Cora and me as well. I've kinda got used to havin' you around. Don't think of going back East again.'

They lapsed into silence. As he took a drink of coffee, Calvin glanced at his companions. They had come through a hard time together. They were solid folk and Ricky and Cora were the future. As regards the present, he was proud to continue as their representative of law and order, the Marshal of Medicine Bend.